BRUSH CREEK COWBOY

CHRISTIAN CONTEMPORARY WESTERN ROMANCE

BRUSH CREEK COWBOYS ROMANCE
BOOK ONE

LIZ ISAACSON

ISBN-13: 978-1638760412

In the quiet misty morning, when the moon has gone to bed,
When the sparrows stop their singing and the sky is clear
and red,
When the summer's ceased its gleaming, when the corn is past
its prime,
When adventure's lost its meaning, I'll be homeward bound
in time.

Bind me not to the pasture. Chain me not to the plow.
Set me free to find my calling and I'll return to you somehow.

If you find it's me you're missing, if you're hoping I'll return,
To your thought I'll soon be list'ning; in the road I'll stop and
turn.
Then the wind will set me racing as my journey nears its end,
And the path I'll be retracing when I'm homeward bound
again.

Bind me not to the pasture. Chain me not to the plow.
Set me free to find my calling and I'll return to you somehow.

In the quiet misty morning when the moon has gone to bed,

*When the sparrows stop their singing, I'll be homeward
bound again."*

*Homeward Bound, ©Marta Keen Thompson, used with
permission*

Chapter 1

Walker Thompson twisted the doorknob with care and stepped into the most glorious summer sunshine Utah had to offer. At least at six-thirty in the morning. He took a deep drag of the sagebrush-scented air and let the worries from the previous night drain from his muscles.

They rushed back within seconds, the way his concerns about his son's night terrors always did. Michael had been particularly restless during the night, and Walker's exhaustion felt like a yoke he couldn't bear.

But bear it he did. Even managed to walk the circumference of his cabin, plucking weedlings from the flower beds that lined the house he shared with his nine-year-old son. It was a ritual he'd started the morning after his wife had passed away, six years ago. The calming, methodical way he could keep things beautiful, keep them uncluttered, allow the pretty flowers room to grow and breathe, had soothed him that day just as it did on this August morning.

Walker didn't live in that house anymore, but in every

successive place he'd moved, he took meticulous care of the yard. It was something he could control.

"Mornin'."

Walker glanced up at the sound of his boss's voice. Landon Edmunds leaned against the fence Walker had built with Michael over the summer, a long piece of straw extending from his mouth.

"Hey, Boss." Walker had known Landon for at least fifteen years, dating all the way back to their rodeo days. Walker had quit the year before Landon had been injured, and he'd worked a couple of ranches in Wyoming before coming to Brush Creek five years ago, when Landon bought it and needed help to make it the premier horse ranch he wanted it to be.

"No one better at breaking horses than you," Landon had told him when he'd called Walker.

Walker hadn't been able to argue, so he'd packed up his son and everything he owned and moved to Utah. And if he was being honest with himself, he'd been happier here than anywhere since his wife had died.

"Goin' to the festival today?" Landon asked.

Walker nodded, his cowboy hat swaying with the motion. He clapped a hand to the top of his head to seat the hat properly. "You?"

"Megan's already got the twins in the tub." Landon chuckled. "She wants you to come to breakfast."

Walker's stomach dropped and rebounded, all within the space of a second. "Tell her thanks, but Michael and I have to get down to town to pick up the cotton candy machine." He wandered over to the fence line and gazed in the same direction as Landon. The red-rock butte in the morning light sent peace straight through his soul. Utah did have gorgeous countryside.

"She won't like that answer," Landon said.

"She just wants to lecture me about dating again," Walker said. He swung his gaze to his long-time friend. "Right?"

"She's worried about you." Landon hooked his green-eyed gaze into Walker's. "So am I."

"I'm just fine." Walker wanted to believe himself, but he'd been unsettled for the last six months—ever since Megan had started needling him about "putting himself out there."

"How's Michael?" Landon asked, going right for the jugular.

Walker exhaled and shuffled his feet. "He's doin' okay." But the truth was, Michael was barely hanging on. Most nine-year-old boys in Brush Creek rode bikes with their friends and went fishing at the water hole on the east edge of town. They slept in tents in each other's backyards and built fires to roast hot dogs.

They didn't live with their widower father out in the middle of nowhere, with only twin two-year-old girls as options for playmates. Oh, and the horses. Michael did love the horses at Brush Creek.

"School starts soon," Landon said, like that would solve the world's problems. It would at least get Michael out of the cabin and into civilization.

Walker didn't know how to answer, so he asked, "Who's Megan got her eye on this time?"

"She didn't say." Landon adjusted his cowboy hat. "She did mention that 'at least five women' would jump at the chance to go out with you." He smiled. "Maybe you can just let her know that she should spread the word that you're available."

"I've always been available," Walker muttered. No one was looking in his direction.

"Not true." Landon cuffed him on the bicep. "See you in town." With that, he strode back toward the homestead calling, "Oh, and Megan's throwing a pool party tomorrow night for everyone. Barbecue and everything."

"Sounds great," Walker yelled after him before turning back to his cabin. He'd helped Landon build the six cowboy cabins that lined the ridge directly across from the homestead. His was the largest, as he was the foreman and had a child. Each of the other cabins housed a single cowboy, all rodeo champions, all expert horsemen. None of them were married or had children.

Walker's mind whirred as he went to wake up his son. Maybe he should open his heart and mind to dating again. Maybe it would be good for Michael to have a mother, be closer to other kids.

Walker didn't want to admit that maybe it would be good for *him* if he found someone to share his life with. He'd loved his wife so much, he didn't think it possible to feel something so profound again.

He pushed open the cabin door and let the light rush in. "Come on, Michael," he called, noting the catch in his voice. After six years, he still missed Libby so deeply it brought his emotion right into his throat. He cleared everything away—his thoughts, his fears, his feelings—and added, "We've got to get down to the festival."

An hour later, he pulled his truck into the parking lot at Oxbow Park. The place was already bustling with activity as vendors and volunteers set up booths, hung signs, and cleared pathways.

"I'll grab the machine," Walker said as he opened his door. "You grab the sacks and twist ties, all right?"

"All right."

Walker took a moment to appreciate his son. He had Walker's shock of black hair and his skin that seemed to soak up the sun's rays. But he looked back at Walker with eyes the exact color of Libby's—hazel, with more brown than green—and the shape of his nose mirrored hers as well. More rounded and flat, whereas Walker sported a long, straight nose.

"Will Tess have the sugar?" Michael asked as Walker lowered the tailgate.

"Supposed to." For some reason, his heart kicked out an extra beat at the thought of Tess Wagner. He'd been friends with Tess since the day she moved to Brush Creek, four years ago. She'd shown up with a two-year-old son and a tragic story about her husband dying in a sheet metal accident, at the very salvage center that he'd owned.

They'd been selling cotton candy and donating the proceeds to the National Widow and Widowers Foundation for the past four summers.

Walker had never known Tess to be late, and she wasn't today either. He found her in their usual location—right across from the lemonade stand—setting up the awning that would protect them from the worst of the sun.

His feet slowed when he saw her, allowing Michael to get ahead of him. Tess had a small flower pinned in her super short blonde hair. She wore a pair of dark blue shorts and a tank top that boasted her slender shoulders and the length of her neck.

Walker's face heated, something that had decidedly never happened when he'd encountered Tess before. He wasn't sure why he was reacting this way to a woman he'd been friends with for years.

Stupid Megan and her stupid insistence about dating, Walker thought as he finally got his feet moving again.

Although, if Walker were really being honest with himself, if he had to start dating again, Tess would be his first choice. He swallowed hard and hefted the cotton candy machine onto the table the town provided.

"Morning," he said and turned his back on Tess so he could get control of himself. At thirty-six years old, he shouldn't have to deal with raging hormones.

"Morning," she chirped. "Michael, Graham's over on the playground. You can go on over, if you want."

Walker glanced up, because he knew his son would look to him for permission before running off. Sure enough, Michael was watching him. "Go on," Walker said with a smile, thinking Tess's seven-year-old son was the perfect friend for Michael.

Maybe he should just ask Tess out. He was grown-up. So was she. She'd been married before. They both had sons. They had a lot in common. Why shouldn't he go out with her?

Why shouldn't I? He tilted his head back and glanced

into the sky, pleading with the Lord to give him a single reason to stay away from Tess Wagner.

Nothing came. Only the richest, bluest sky stared back.

At the very least, it would get Megan Edmunds off his back about "putting himself out there."

Determined in his plan to leave the festival that evening with a date on the horizon, he was finally able to relax in Tess's presence.

Chapter 2

Tess Wagner shivered though the late-summer sun should've warmed her all the way through. Beside her, Walker seemed to be sweating, and almost everyone who came up to their booth looked like they were melting.

She kept her smile in place, kept the cardboard tubes circling in the spun sugar, kept working until four o'clock, when the booths closed in preparation for the nightly entertainment that culminated the town's apricot festival.

Working next to Walker for the past six hours had been the sweetest kind of torture. He smelled like musky cologne and fresh air, and she wanted to bottle him up and take him home with her. Tess had been watching Walker with new eyes since the firefighter's pancake breakfast over the Fourth of July. She'd seen him in a different light then, wearing an apron and flipping pancakes, laughing with the other volunteer firefighters, pouring syrup for his son. Something inside her had shifted then, and she hadn't known how to deal with it.

She did know she wanted to take things with him out of the friendship zone. She just wasn't sure how, or if that was even fair to him. Or to her. Or to Graham and Michael. They'd all already lost so much.

She finished cleaning the cotton candy machine and sighed as she looked out across the park. Oxbow Park was Tess's absolute favorite place in the world. She lived just down the street, and she loved spending quiet afternoons walking the banks of the stream that flowed from one end of the park to the other. Loved watching the younger moms chat while sitting on benches while their little kids ran and played. Loved bringing Graham here for weeknight picnics all summer long, her delicious German chocolate cake a favorite for them both.

The park swarmed with people now, as it seemed like all of Brush Creek's nine thousand citizens had come out for the festival. The other vendors started packing up, but Tess fell into the chair at the rear of her and Walker's booth. "I'm tired," she said.

"Yeah." Walker didn't even glance over his shoulder to her. He continued to flip paper money, counting it silently. "We made more this year than any other year." He turned and faced her, a wide smile on his handsome face. He made jeans and a T-shirt seem sexy, and something about the strength in his soul sang to Tess's.

She returned his grin, glad for someone so wonderful in her life. Her friendship with Walker meant a lot to her— and the cause they both supported each year meant even more. Did she dare risk their easy relationship for a chance at something more? Indecision and worry gnawed at her, making her already upset stomach downright angry.

"You don't look so great," he said, coming closer and crouching to look right into her face. "You should go lie down."

She bristled at the suggestion even as a fair amount of heat enveloped her at his near proximity. She seized onto it and tried to use it to make herself warm. "I don't want to miss the band," she said. "Besides, Graham will be disappointed."

"I can take 'im," Walker said. "I'll drop him off before I head up the canyon."

Without thinking, Tess reached out and traced her fingers down the side of Walker's face. She pulled back at the fire in his skin, at the pure electricity that zipped through her hand, at the shock traveling through his eyes.

He straightened and backed away from her as far as the table behind him would allow. She wasn't sure if she should apologize or not, so she remained mute, hoping the heat from touching him would evaporate into the sky. It didn't. It only amped up, roaring into a furious firestorm inside her veins.

"I wanted to ask you something," he said, his eyes trained on the ground.

"Okay." Her voice sounded like she'd swallowed frogs, but still Walker didn't look at her.

"Megan says I need to—" He cleared his throat and turned around. He stuffed the money into a bank pouch before saying, "I was wondering if maybe you'd like to go to dinner with me sometime."

Tess stood, thankful her legs didn't wobble. She wasn't sure why she was so tired today. She hadn't had a chemotherapy treatment in ages, and her last body scan had confirmed that she was still cancer-free.

She joined Walker at the table, definitely closer than she normally stood, but far enough away to be respectable to anyone passing by. "How did you know?"

"Know what?" He glanced at her but didn't let his gaze settle on hers before focusing on the money again.

"That I was hoping you'd ask me out." Feeling brave and courageous and all the things she usually wasn't, she put her hand over his.

"Dad." Michael raced up to the booth, and Tess slid her fingers away from Walker's, shifted away from him, and started boxing up the leftover sugar and plastic bags.

"What?" Walker's attention went to his son.

"Can I sit by Troy and Ian for the concert?"

Several beats of silence followed, and Tess turned back as Graham returned to the stand. She ran her hand over his hair and smiled. "Hey baby."

She faced Walker. "Troy's last name is Munk," she said. "He's ten. Ian is his little brother. He's seven. Their family owns the bakery." Walker trained his eyes on her, curiosity dancing in the dark depths of them. She shrugged. "It would probably be fine. Graham and Ian are friends."

He nodded and looked back at Michael. "Take Graham with you then. What do you guys want for dinner?"

"Troy says the food trucks will be here in an hour. Corny's is coming." Michael looked so hopeful, and Graham loved the corndogs and twister fries from the Corny's truck too.

Walker nodded and fished a twenty-dollar bill from the pouch. "Get Graham whatever he wants too. Check in with me so I know where you are and who you're with. We're not doin' sleepovers tonight. It's church tomorrow."

Michael grinned, plucked the money from his father's fingers, and he and Graham raced back toward the pair of boys waiting for them near the pavilion. Tess watched her son go, a rush of love filling her that she was able to provide this life for him. A slower, more carefree life than the one she'd had in Salt Lake.

"So," Walker said, his fingers sliding down her forearm to capture hers. "I guess it's just you and me tonight."

Tess shivered again, this time for a completely different reason than before. She gazed up into Walker's face, relieved when she saw a blur of emotion in his eyes too. She felt so tangled up, she was sure she'd never unravel the mixture of feelings inside.

"I guess so," she managed to say. "But I do *not* want to eat a corndog from a food truck."

Walker tipped his head back and laughed, easing some of the tension in Tess's muscles. "They're *gourmet* corn-dogs," he said. "But all right. What about heading over to the chuck wagon dinner? I bought tickets for Michael and me, and he's obviously not coming...."

A tremor of terror tripped through Tess. Would people start gossiping about them if they went to the fundraising dinner together? What would her chocolate club think?

Why did she care?

They'd worked the booth together all day, and she hadn't worried about that. Everyone in town already knew they were friends. No one would probably think twice about them going to the chuck wagon dinner together. It wasn't exactly romantic, and they wouldn't exactly have any privacy.

"Sure," Tess said. "Do you think they'll give me two pieces of that grilled corn on the cob? I love that stuff."

He released her hand and reached for the top of the awning. "I'll let you have mine," he said, and a glow she hadn't felt in years warmed Tess from the inside out.

––––––––

As THEY TOOK down the awning and Walker headed back to his truck with the rented cotton candy machine, Tess fretted. First, about going out with Walker. Though it was what she wanted, she wasn't sure it was smart. She normally studied things out, prayed about them, considered all angles, before doing something.

She hadn't done that here. He'd asked; she'd said yes. Not only that, but she'd practically told him she'd been *desperate* for him to ask her out for a while now. She shook her head. She hadn't said too much, though holding the man's hand had definitely conveyed *something*.

Second, her thoughts kept flying back to Brandon, the husband she'd lost to a terrible accident only five years ago. Graham had been two years old, and Tess had tried to move on with her life in Salt Lake City. She'd found it impossible though, surrounded by all the same friends, her family, all the employees at the scrap metal salvage.

So she'd sold it. Moved to a remote town with more livestock than people. Cut hair a couple days a week just to avoid boredom. Hosted monthly chocolate parties at her house. Raised Graham by herself. Endured her cancer treatments with the help of a few close friends.

"There you are."

Tess glanced up from the bench where she'd sat to find those friends standing in front of her. "Paige." She grinned and rose to embrace the brunette. "Alison, hey. How did the fish pond go?"

Alison waved her hand. "Just fine. The pastor was a big hit." A honey-haired blonde, Alison was the preacher's wife, at least a decade older than Tess. She found that after her husband's death, she no longer fit in the twenty-something crowd. She related better to older women, and Tess was the youngest of the group at thirty-four.

"How'd the cotton candy do this year?" Shirley asked. She owned a pie shop in town that shared space with the bakery, which her son operated.

"Great," Tess said. "Walker said we made more this year than any other year." She glanced over her shoulder to see where he'd gone. She couldn't see him.

"What are you doing now?" Paige asked.

Tess shrugged. "Graham is off getting dinner with Troy and Ian, so Walker and I are going to go to the chuck wagon dinner." She felt scandalous and she couldn't quite meet any of her friends' eyes. "What about you guys?"

"Food truck rally," Alison said. "Oh, there's Bob. I better go." She patted Tess's arm the way she usually did. "Good to see you! Chocolate club on Wednesday night?"

"I have this new triple-chocolate cookie recipe," Paige singsonged, and Shirley said, "I'm bringing my chocolate crème Oreo pie."

"Wednesday," Tess confirmed as her friends bustled

away, leaving her alone on the bench once more. The park around her buzzed with activity, but she felt isolated, abandoned.

At least until Walker returned a few minutes later. "Everything's loaded up. Dinner doesn't start for another hour." He collapsed onto the bench next to her, and every cell in her body wanted to take his hand in hers and steal his quiet strength. "You wanna walk for a while? Then maybe we can stop by your place to clean up before the chuck wagon thing."

"Can we go down by the stream?" Tess asked.

Walker slipped his hand in hers and stood up, pulling her after him. "We can go wherever you want, beautiful." He grinned and squeezed her fingers. "You lead the way."

And for the first time since her husband had died, for the first time since she'd been diagnosed with breast cancer, for the first time since she'd started losing her hair, Tess felt beautiful. All because the gorgeous cowboy smiling down at her said so.

CHAPTER 3

Walker wasn't entirely sure why his heart galloped the way it did, or why he felt like the trees had suddenly grown eyes. All he knew was that Tess had said yes. That Tess had been thinking about him too. That Tess wanted to go out with him.

He hadn't felt wanted in a long time. Necessary, sure. Michael needed him at home. Landon needed him on the horse ranch. But *needed* and *wanted* were two very different things, as Walker was suddenly keenly aware of.

"You sure you're feeling okay?" he asked as they sauntered along the banks of the stream, leaving the crowds back by the parking lot, the stage, and the playground.

"I'm tired," Tess confessed.

"When's the last time you went to the doctor?" Walker tried to make his voice sound soothing, non-judgmental. They'd talked about her health before; this wasn't anything new.

"June," she said. "My scans were all clear."

"Ah, yes. I remember," he said. "You made about a hundred tacos to celebrate."

She nudged him with her shoulder. "I like tacos."

"So do I," he said. "But no one needs a hundred."

"They all got eaten." She looked at him, and he got lost in her blue-gray eyes for a moment. "This town is really good at celebrating with each other."

"It helped that you set up that big table in your driveway."

"How many did you eat?"

Walker grinned at her. "Probably six. Maybe eight."

She laughed, the pretty little sound of it infecting Walker's bloodstream. As if the summer evening wasn't already hot enough, now Walker found himself roasting from the inside out.

"I don't suppose they'll have peanut butter and jelly sandwiches on the chuck wagon," she said.

He stepped with her, the ultra slow pace almost hard to maintain. "Peanut butter and jelly? I wouldn't think so. Why?"

"That's what I want for my final meal," she said.

Walker's heart stuttered. "Tess." He stopped and twisted toward her. "Your final meal?"

"I just—" She glanced over his shoulder and then locked her eyes on his.

"You're not dying," he said.

"We're all dying, Walker."

He shook his head, not quite sure what to say. "But tonight's not your final meal."

"Probably not." A ghost of a smile wafted across her face. He had the strongest urge to pull her into his chest and hold her tight. So he did. And oh, holding her felt magical, like she fit against him and should always be there. How he hadn't known this before tonight was a mystery to him.

"Do you need to go back to the doctor?" he whispered.

She clung to him, a slight tremor traveling through her shoulders. "No, I'm fine. I just spent all day in the sun. I'm just tired."

"We don't have to go to dinner," he said. "I'm sure that wood-fire pizza truck will be here tonight. I can grab us something and we can take it back to your house."

The thought of spending a more private evening with Tess sent Walker's heart right back to galloping. With her cheek pressed against his chest, he was sure she'd feel it. Sure she'd know of his erratic feelings.

He'd spent five extra minutes loading the cotton candy machine, coaching himself to not act like a hormonal teenager. But he'd been out of the dating game for so long, he'd forgotten all the rules. Things had changed so much in the past twenty years, he didn't even think the same rules existed.

He'd even gone so far as to consider calling Megan. *Megan!* The woman who'd basically gotten him into this mess. Without her, he wouldn't have even been thinking about asking someone out.

"Tess?" he asked when she didn't answer. "Pizza or chuck wagon?"

"I don't want you to miss the dinner," she said.

He pulled back and looked into her face. "They already got my money. It doesn't matter if I go or not." He could read the exhaustion on her face, and if he were being honest, the same tiredness existed in his very soul. So he said, "Let me find the boys and give them my phone. Then we'll go. I can run back over to get the pizza when the trucks show up."

She nodded without argument—a testament to her fatigue—and he released her. They returned to the bench she'd been sitting on earlier, and he left her there to go find Michael and Graham.

"Boys," he said when he found them. "Tess isn't feeling very well. I'm going to take her home." He extended his phone to his son. "I want you guys to take this. Text me or call me if you need anything."

Michael took the phone almost reverently. "Dad?"

"She's just tired." He tousled the boy's hair. "You have the money for corndogs and fries. Now you have a way to communicate with me. When the concert ends, come on back to Graham's." He glanced at Tess's son, finding her same eyes, the same smattering of freckles across the child's nose. "You guys can stay together, right?"

"Yes, sir," Graham said, and Walker smiled at him. "Michael?"

"Yeah, sure, Dad."

"We'll stay with them too, Mister Thompson," Troy said. "My dad will be here in a few minutes."

Walker nodded. "He can text me too." He wished the man was there now, so Walker could make sure it was all right to leave the boys for the evening. He focused on Michael. "You'll be okay?"

Michael's chest swelled. "Dad, I'm not a baby."

He thunked Michael on the shoulder. "I know you're not. Stay together. Get something to eat. Let me know when you're on your way back to Graham's. It'll be dark, and I'll come out and meet you."

"All right," Michael drawled in that western twang he'd learned on the cattle ranch in Evanston.

That settled, Walker wove through the crowds at Oxbow, separate rivers of unease splashing through him. He spotted Landon and changed course mid-step. "Hey," he said. The twins were sleeping in their double-wide stroller while Megan relaxed on the bench beside them. He glanced at Megan, who trained her eyes on him. He swore she could see right into his mind, and he looked away.

"I'm leavin' Michael and Graham here." He pointed back toward where they were tossing a football with the Munk boys. "Can you maybe keep an eye on them tonight? I gave Michael my phone, but I wasn't able to talk to an adult."

"Where are you goin'?" Landon asked.

"Tess isn't feeling well," he said. "I'm gonna make sure she gets home all right."

Megan rose. "Tess Wagner?"

Walker worked hard not to roll his eyes. "It's nothing, Megan."

"Which means it's something." She clapped her hands together in delight. "Did you ask her out?"

Walker trained his gaze on Megan, a blip of satisfaction stealing through him when she flinched the slightest bit. "As a matter of fact, I did. We were going to go to the chuck wagon dinner, but she's not feeling up to it."

She cocked her head. "But you for real asked her out?"

Walker sighed and looked back at Landon. "Can you keep an eye on them? We'll have Tess's phone."

"I don't know her number," Landon said.

"I've got it," Megan said, absolute glee on her face. "And oh, poor Brighton will be so heartbroken to hear you're going out with someone else."

"Brighton Kallas?" Walker asked. He wasn't sure if he should be horrified or relieved he'd dodged that bullet.

"She thinks you're *soo* handsome." Megan giggled, her fingers flying over her phone.

Walker snatched it from her fingers. "I don't want you texting every female in the county about this."

Megan made a grab for her phone, but Walker kept it easily out of her reach. "I'm not texting every female in the county."

"Megan," Walker warned.

She smiled warmly at him. "Walker." She brushed at her eyes, all playfulness gone. "I'm so happy for you."

Landon scoffed. "It's not like he's engaged."

Megan shoved him in the chest. "Getting out there again is really hard, Landon. You of all people should know that."

"Yeah, well," Landon muttered. "Can we not make a big deal out of it? I think Walker would appreciate that."

Walker nodded. "I would, actually."

"Can I have my phone back?" Megan folded her arms, that grin stuck to her face.

"Promise not to text any women about this?"

"What about Landon's sister? Can I tell her? She'll be thrilled."

Disbelief snaked through Walker. "You've told someone I've never met about my pathetic love life?"

Landon chuckled. "If there's someone more meddlesome than my wife, it's my sister."

Walker shook his head. "I can't believe this." He held out Megan's phone.

"Oh, you like it." She took the phone and stretched up to kiss him on the cheek. "Good for you, Walker. Go have fun."

"She's probably going to fall asleep on the couch," he muttered before turning away.

"But you'll be with her!" Megan called after him.

———

When Walker returned with the pizza, Tess was indeed fast asleep on the couch. His own weariness allowed him to sink into the armchair next to her, turn the TV volume down another couple of notches so as not to disturb her, and eat a few slices.

He was just starting to doze himself with the thought of *This is the most unromantic date I've ever been on* when someone knocked on the door.

He shot out of the chair like he'd been launched by a cannon. A quick glance to Tess confirmed that she slept like the dead. He cracked the door just enough to see who stood on the other side.

A dark-haired woman he recognized from church. "Oh, hello, Paige."

She scanned him from boots to cowboy hat, taking in as much of him as the slit in the doorway would allow. "Walker Thompson?" She tried to see past him. "What are you doing here?"

"Tess wasn't feeling well. I just made sure she got home okay." A hum of discomfort seethed beneath his skin. "My son wanted to go to the concert with Graham, so I'm just waiting here for them."

Paige appraised him. "Weren't you guys going to go to the chuck wagon dinner?"

He wondered how she knew that, but just said, "Yes, but we decided not to."

She lifted a paper plate. "Oh, well, I brought Tess one of her favorites."

Walker took the plate and stared at the sandwich. "PB&J?"

"Not just *any* PB&J," Paige said with a smile. "That's white chocolate peanut butter and freshly made apricot jam."

"I'm sure she'll love it." Walker gave Paige his best smile. "I'll make sure she gets it."

Paige gave him a knowing look, though just what she knew, he wasn't sure. "All right then." She turned and went down the steps, leaving Walker to wonder why she'd knocked if she'd expected Tess to be at the chuck wagon dinner.

He didn't have room in his brain to riddle it all out. He sighed and closed the door, nearly dropping the gourmet sandwich—if such a thing existed—when he came toe-to-toe with Tess. "Who was that?" she asked.

"Paige." He extended the sandwich toward her. "Brought you dinner."

A smile painted life back into Tess's face and sent a shiver of wanting through Walker. "I also made it back with the pizza."

"I saw that." She took the sandwich into her kitchen and padded back into the living room. "Sorry I fell asleep." She curled into the corner of the couch, but Walker didn't know where to put himself. He wanted to cuddle up right next to her, but something about it didn't feel quite right.

"It's not a problem," he said. "I may have started to doze myself." He moved toward the armchair just as she patted the cushion next to her. He changed course and sat beside her, his position saying *I'm definitely interested but I'm not going to make the first move.*

Didn't matter. Tess did by reaching out and twining her fingers through his. She shifted away from the armrest, replacing it with Walker's shoulder. "You haven't dated since Libby's death, have you?" she asked.

"No, ma'am."

She giggled. "I'm thirty-four, Walker. Don't call me ma'am."

"Yes, ma'am."

She swatted his arm and he added his laughter to hers. "Have you dated since Brandon died?"

"No," she whispered.

"Why do you think that is?" he asked. "I mean, why don't we—can't we—move on?"

"I've moved on in other ways."

So had Walker. He'd just never taken the time to think about them, sort through them. "I guess I have too," he said. "But in some things, I still haven't let go."

"What things?"

He drew in a deep breath and let it leak slowly out, contemplating how to articulate his feelings. "I think the biggest one my mother worries about is the fact that I haven't been back to visit Libby's grave."

"Not even once?"

"Not even once." The thought of going there, to "visit" her, made Walker feel put together wrong. She wasn't there. She didn't even know if he came or stayed away.

"So I'm not sure if that means I've let go or I haven't." Walker leaned his head back against the couch. "I'm sure my mother could tell you all about it."

The mood lightened, and she asked, "Where is your family?"

"California. Born and raised."

"And somehow you became a cowboy instead of a surfer. Interesting."

"The ocean has never called to me," he explained. "Fresh air, and mountains, and working with the earth. That's what I've always liked."

"It suits you."

"You've never even seen what I do."

"Oh, I don't know about that."

Walker shifted away from her and their eyes met. "What does that mean?"

"It means you were a professional rodeo star at one point, Mister Thompson, and YouTube has a lot of videos on it."

His heart battered his ribcage. "You looked up footage of me riding?" He wasn't quite sure if he should be flattered or not. The warmth flowing through him urged him toward flattery though.

"Maybe once or twice." Her voice sounded so false that Walker tipped his chin toward the ceiling and laughed.

"Once or twice."

"Fine, a dozen or so times. You were great. Pro for five years. Why'd you quit?"

He lifted his arm and she sank right into his side. He secured her in place and watched the flickering lights on the television. "It was time. Libby was pregnant. The traveling was too much to bring a family along, and I'd be gone too long to leave them behind."

"You ever regret retiring?"

"No," he said firmly. "Sometimes I miss the circuit, sure. But I've got Michael, and I still have a taste of the rodeo life with Landon and Justin and Ted. We all rode the rodeo circuit together."

"Sounds great."

Walker didn't tell her that though he was surrounded by loved ones, he still felt lonelier than ever—except for the past day. With her, he didn't feel so isolated.

"You should come up to the ranch sometime," he said. "Bring Graham. Maybe he'd like to ride or something."

"I was going to ask you about that," she said.

"Oh yeah?"

"Well, not that, specifically."

"What, then?"

"Graham and Michael seem to get along really great, and I was thinking...."

Walker waited for her to continue.

"I was thinking maybe when school starts in a couple of weeks, you'll send Michael home with Graham a few days a week."

Confusion drew Walker's eyebrows into a crease. "I'm not sure—"

"There's fall soccer signups happening at the rec center right now, and Graham's dying to play, but he wants Michael to do it with him. So they could go together. I could take them. You could come down from the ranch whenever you're done working."

"I don't need a nanny," he said, his first defense slamming the door on all of her suggestions.

She laughed. "Walker Thompson, you are so stubborn." She lifted herself out of his embrace and looked him square in the face. "I'm not looking to be your nanny." Her gaze was clear and her meaning as plain as day.

He cleared his throat as his gaze dropped to her full lips. He yanked his eyes back to hers, but he'd already thought about kissing her and he couldn't go back now. "What are you doing then?" he managed to ask through a dry throat.

"Maybe a carpool arrangement," she said with one sexy shrug of her shoulder. "You stop by in the morning and pick up the boys and take them to school. Michael can come home with Graham. They can go to soccer together, be boys, go fishing in the stream at Oxbow. Whatever. He can't be getting much of that at Brush Creek."

He wasn't getting any of that at Brush Creek. Walker's resolve slipped the teensiest bit. "A carpool?" he asked. "So we're soccer moms now?"

She leaned in, closer and closer, until Walker had to close his eyes or go crosseyed. Her lips brushed his cheek. "You're definitely not a soccer mom," she whispered. "I can bring Michael home whenever you say. Maybe I'll even bring you dinner sometimes, like you said. Visit the ranch, like you suggested."

Walker liked the idea of Tess on the horse ranch. Liked it very much. "All right," he found himself saying.

"All right," she echoed, retreating and tucking herself back into his side. "This is a win-win, Walker, trust me. I like to sleep in, Michael gets to have time with friends, and you don't have to worry so much."

"Who says I was worried?"

"Megan," Tess said, and boy, if that didn't make Walker's blood boil.

CHAPTER 4

Tess didn't make it to church the next morning, but she sent Graham with Paige's family. Walker texted her during most of the sermon, but he didn't stop by afterward. A pin pushed into her heart, though she didn't know why. They'd spent a few hours on her couch, talking. It wasn't the most romantic event as far as first dates went. It probably bored him to listen to her talk about her two older sisters, or the many and varied food rules she had.

He had laughed a lot when she'd detailed those. "No cookies without milk?" he'd asked. "I guess that one's okay. But why can't you have cake without ice cream?"

She'd tried to explain her reasoning, but in the end, he'd simply said, "Whatever you want, beautiful," and gone to meet the boys so they didn't have to walk home in the dark by themselves.

School didn't start for another three weeks, and Tess found herself trying to think of ways to get Walker down the canyon so she could see him. It was only a fifteen-minute drive up to the ranch, but she couldn't just stop by. How would she even explain that?

I took a wrong turn....

She shook her head as she stirred Graham's macaroni and cheese. "All done," she announced, scooping some of the very orange food into a bowl for him. "Spoon or fork?"

"Spoon," he said, and she produced one from the silverware drawer.

"How was church?" she asked.

"Boring."

She laughed and reached for her phone as it chimed. Walker's text read, *I'd like to see you again. Dinner tomorrow night? We can take the boys with us.*

Her attention on her phone became singular as she typed *Sure, what time?* She stared at the words. Too forward? Too enthusiastic? Not enthusiastic enough? Should she use an exclamation point?

Sure! What time?

She shook her head, wondering when dating had become so dang complicated. In the end, she went without punctuation at all.

Sure what time

It looked so dysfunctional after she sent it, but she couldn't take it back now.

Six-thirty?

Sounds great.

She pulled down a cookbook, her mind set on baking something chocolatey and delicious now that she'd gotten in a few more hours of sleep—and had a date with the cowboy of her dreams on the horizon.

You feeling better? Walker texted before she even cracked the spine of the cookbook.

A lot better, she confirmed. *Making something ooey gooey and full of chocolate.*

Sounds dangerous.

I'll bring you some.

He didn't text back, and worry exploded through Tess. Her stomach churned, and every recipe she looked at sounded disgusting. In the end, she left her phone sitting on the kitchen counter, and said to Graham, "I'm going to take a bath. Holler if you need anything."

By four o'clock, she was washed, perfumed, and all done up. She had a chocolate cheesecake cooling in the refrigerator. Now all she needed was an excuse to get up to Brush Creek.

Not an excuse for herself—she knew why she wanted to go.

She didn't need an explanation for Walker—she said she'd bring him a treat.

No, she needed a reason for Graham, who wasn't stupid just because he was young. For Paige, who had invited her to dinner at six. For Shirley and Alison, who would surely ask endless questions once they found out about the hand-holding and cheek-kissing with Walker Thompson.

Tess was surprised her friends hadn't called yet. She gave all the credit to Paige, who probably wanted to get the juicy details for herself before sharing them with the other girls. "And that's why she invited us to dinner," Tess said aloud.

"What, Mom?" Graham's attention flickered from the cartoons in front of him.

"Nothing, baby. Just talkin' to myself." She reached

over and slung her arm around him. "Hey, you wanna go up to Brush Creek this afternoon? Maybe see what Michael's doing?"

"Yeah, sure." Graham didn't seem suspicious or concerned about this irregular Sunday activity. And why would he be? He probably wanted to play with Michael's dogs and run through the fields.

"Walker said you might be able to ride a horse. Would you like that?"

Graham reached for the remote and switched off the TV. "Maybe. I've never ridden a horse before."

Tess smiled fondly at her son. "We'll just see then. Go get your shoes on."

Graham scampered away to do what she asked, and Tess gathered her wits and thumbed out a message to Paige that said she couldn't make it to dinner. She didn't explain why, but she knew Paige would ask.

Sure enough, the next text asked her how she felt, and maybe she could send Graham.

Tess decided to get the truth out of the way. No sense in hiding it from her best friends. Paige would find out sooner or later, and it wasn't like Tess needed to hide a budding relationship. She pressed the call button and headed into the kitchen. Paige picked up before the first ring ended. "Tess, what's going on? Are you okay?"

Tess laughed. "Paige, I'm fine. What's got you so worked up?"

"Well, I brought you a killer PB&J last night, and you were asleep. Then you send Graham to church alone, and now you can't come to dinner. *Something's* going on."

"First, thank you for the sandwich. I ate it for breakfast,

and it was the best PB&J I've ever had. I totally want that again for my last meal."

Paige took her declaration of last meals much better than Walker had, sending a laugh through the line. "You'll need to figure out how to get your hands on some of that white chocolate peanut butter then."

"I bet I can find it online."

"You can find anything online."

"Online shopping is essential when you live in a small town," Tess said, her tone only slightly defensive. Tess liked certain cleaners, and throw pillows that actually filled the shams, and having lots of clothing options. She adored Brush Creek, from the quaint parks, the old-town brick buildings on Main Street, and the friendly people who'd welcomed her with open arms. But the shopping wasn't stellar.

Others like Paige stuck to what they could find in the aisles of Preston's Furniture, and Lynn's Market, and the single department store at the end of the block.

"Second?" Paige prompted.

"Second, I'm...I can't come to dinner because I'm going up to Brush Creek."

Paige gave her two seconds of silence before squealing. "I knew it! I knew something was going on with Walker Thompson when he opened your front door last night. Alison is going to owe me so many cookies."

"It's just so Graham can play with Michael. It's such a beautiful day, and we're all cooped up here."

"Sure," Paige said with more sarcasm than air in the word. "And Michael's *stunning father* has nothing to do with this *sudden* and *unexpected* trip up the canyon, right?"

"Stunning?" Tess laughed. "I wouldn't describe Walker as stunning." She leaned against the counter and watched for Graham to come back downstairs. "Maybe gorgeous, or handsome, or dignified. Exciting, maybe. Sexy, sure. Strong, definitely. But stunning? Not sure it fits."

Paige laughed and laughed, even when Tess said she had to go because Graham had returned, ready to go. Just before she turned to go up the canyon to Brush Creek, Tess got a text from Paige: *I want details when you get back tonight! Have fun!*

With her insides so knotted, she wasn't sure fun was on the horizon. She crested the hill that ended at the sprawling Brush Creek Horse Ranch. On her right lay the large homestead. The house was rustic, but obviously upscale, with a low brick fence surrounding it. The landscaping was meticulous; the towering trees had leaves that fluttered in the breeze.

Horse barns and sheds, training facilities and the covered horse arena stretched beyond that. Tess's prize sat on the left, where a lane led to another frontage road that ran in front of the six cowboy cabins. Walker's sat in the middle and was by far the largest.

She found him and Michael in the yard, throwing a football back and forth. When Michael caught sight of her car, he jogged toward them. Walker pressed the football between both of his hands and stayed in the middle of the emerald-green lawn, his eyes bright and watchful.

A pair of dogs panted in the shade on the front porch, one a black lab and one yellow. They both stood as Graham leapt from the barely-stopped car and ran toward Michael.

They both continued toward the dogs, whose tails wagged like Graham had shown up just to see them.

Tess got out of the car more slowly and took precious seconds to collect the cheesecake from the backseat. She wielded the dessert like a shield as she navigated the distance between herself and Walker.

"This should be in the fridge," she said. "I can run it in, if you want."

Walker licked his lips, which completely distracted Tess. "Sure, let's go." Walker led her inside his cabin while the boys wrestled with the dogs and threw a wiffle ball that the black lab always beat the yellow one to.

"Don't mind Bruce and Wayne. They don't bite."

"Bruce and Wayne? Like Batman?" She giggled as she stepped into the blessed air conditioning. She wasn't expecting the natural wood walls, the feature wall lined with bricks and sporting a fireplace. A piano stood against one wall, with a television on top of that, with a couch facing them both. The hardwood on the floor felt old and new at the same time.

The kitchen had stainless steel appliances, stylish tile, and dark oak cabinets. She whistled through her teeth. The soft gray on the walls and black pulls completed the look, tying everything together.

"Wow," she said. "This place is really nice."

"Built it myself." He opened the fridge and stepped back.

"No kidding?" She slid the cheesecake onto an empty shelf, noting that there were several.

"Well, Landon and I built it. We built them all when I first moved here." He let the fridge swing closed. "He bought all this extra land so he could house horsemen here, on-site."

"So the other cabins are full?"

"Yep. Five cowboys, plus me." He leaned against the countertop. "I'm the foreman."

"Of course you are." She grinned up at him, hoping her words sounded flirtatious enough. "You like chocolate, right?" She ran her hands up and down her arms, suddenly nervous and cold.

"Who doesn't like chocolate?"

She giggled. "Believe it or not, I've met a few people."

"Mutants." He chuckled and gave her a sly smile that sent her heart rate skyrocketing. "I've heard you host a monthly chocolate club."

"Life is short," Tess said. "No sense in wasting a single day without chocolate."

He nodded toward the fridge. "So can we have it now, or do we have to wait?"

"I thought maybe you'd show me around the ranch first." She took a single step closer to him, reaching out and tiptoeing her fingers up his chest to his collar, where she fiddled with the buttons on his polo. "I like this shirt. I don't see you in much more than a T-shirt or a white shirt for church."

He nodded toward the front door. "Well, you'll have to stop by more often then. My wardrobe certainly has more than that in it." He stepped toward the door and she went with him, almost desperate to be in the same space as him. The strength of her emotions sent shock and fear through her, but she went anyway.

She'd only made it a few steps down the front sidewalk

before she blinked and the world didn't come back to full color. Another blink, and the scenery around her went fuzzy along the edges.

"Walker," she managed to say. He turned and the panic in his beautiful, midnight eyes was the last thing she saw before she fainted.

————

She woke up on an unfamiliar couch, with strange smells surrounding her, and a very hot hand touching her face. Voices echoed in her head—male voices. One female.

In those soft moments before she was all the way awake, before anyone noticed that she'd partially regained consciousness, she knew she needed to get back to the doctor in Evanston as soon as possible.

Dread settled like lead in her stomach, and her first thought was *What will happen to Graham when I die?*

She groaned, tears flooding her eyes as the ache in her soul radiated through her whole body. *Dear Lord, please help me*, she begged. *Please don't leave my son alone in this world.*

"It's okay." Walker's handsome face appeared in her line of sight. "Tess, you're just fine. Tell me what hurts."

"My head." She tried to sit up, but he gently pressed one hand to her shoulder to keep her prostrate on the couch. "Did I fall?"

"I caught you."

Of course he did. "I need to get to the hospital," she said. "Will you take me to Evanston?"

Though he'd confessed that he hadn't been back to

Evanston since his wife's death, there was no hesitation when he said, "Of course. Let me arrange care for the boys."

Tess let him go, her eyes drifting closed again. She didn't understand why this was happening now, the very day after she'd decided to branch out of her comfort zone and go out with a man for the first time in years. Was it a sign?

Tess dismissed the thought. She didn't believe in signs. She embraced hope for the future. She had faith in—

She stopped there.

She had faith. A sense of peace filled her, and though she didn't know if things would work out or not, she knew there was a Master in charge of everything.

And she had faith in Him.

CHAPTER 5

"No, I need to go to Evanston," Tess said from Walker's passenger seat.

"It's too far," he said. "They can at least make sure you're stable here." He pulled into the hospital in Vernal, only a forty-five minute drive from Brush Creek, as compared to the three-hour drive to Evanston. He'd wondered why her oncologist was in Evanston instead of Salt Lake, where she'd moved from. Even Rock Springs would've shaved a whole hour off the drive for her appointments and treatments.

"Come on." He flipped the truck into park and hurried around the front of the vehicle to be there for Tess. He'd carried her from where she'd collapsed on his front sidewalk to Megan and Landon's house, and then to his truck once it was decided that the boys would stay at Brush Creek, in Landon's basement. Megan had been blowing up air beds and digging sleeping bags out of the closet when Walker had left.

He wasn't worried about Michael and Graham. No, all

of his care and concern rested on Tess. She'd dozed on and off as he made the drive toward civilization, and he didn't like the gray color of her face.

He swept her into his arms, glad when she didn't protest but instead wrapped her arms around his neck and clung to him. He breathed in the soft scent of her skin, which smelled like baby powder and fresh cotton, and hurried through the automatic doors of the emergency room.

"I need help here," he said and people seemed to materialize from the very walls themselves. "She has breast cancer," he explained to a man who brought forward a wheelchair. "Her treatments have all been done in Evanston." He leaned down. "Who's your doctor, Tess?"

"Lipman," she said. "Sylvia Lipman."

Walker nodded at the nurse, who moved away with Tess. He watched helplessly as the big plastic door swung closed behind them, removing her from his sight. Everything inside him deflated, and he wondered what in the world he was doing. If this had been like every other Sunday, he'd be sitting down to dinner with Landon and Megan, not a thought about Tess anywhere near his mind.

Of course, that was also a lie. Tess had been on his mind for the past six months, even before he consciously knew it. Now he was pacing in a hospital waiting room, his nerves frayed after an hour-long nightmare where one of his best friends had fainted. Before, he would've heard about her fainting spell and texted her to see if she was okay, but it wouldn't have disrupted his entire evening.

Best friends rang in his mind as someone said, "Sir, can we get some information from you?"

"What?" He blinked and looked down at the nurse. "Oh, yeah. As much as I can tell you, sure." He stepped over to the check-in desk and filled out as much of the forms as he could, which admittedly wasn't much. He didn't know Tess's social security number. Or her insurance information. Or her emergency contact. He ended up putting himself for that and thought she could just change it later.

He finished and found a chair in the corner, swiping off his hat and rubbing his hands through his hair as the events of the day washed through him. Pastor Peters had spoken about staying close to the Lord through trials.

Walker had learned that when Libby died. He hadn't been much of a church-goer before that, though he tagged along with Libby if he was in town. After her death, he found solace and comfort in the music he heard at church. The sermons weren't always rousing, but as soon as the choir stood up, Walker's soul was awakened.

Before Libby's death, she'd requested he play the song *Homeward Bound* at her funeral. He'd practiced it for hours on the piano though he could sit down and sight-read almost anything. No one had sung, but the words still hung in Walker's mind.

Bind me not to the pasture. Chain me not to the plow.

Set me free to find my calling and I'll return to you somehow.

Was the Lord calling Tess home too? Now?

Frustration rose through Walker. It didn't seem fair that he'd have to suffer through the deaths of two wives.

"She's not your wife," he whispered to himself, relieved no one sat close enough to hear him talking to himself. He didn't even love her; he hadn't even kissed her. Why then, did his heart feel like it was cracking in half?

Twenty minutes passed before someone came to get Walker. He jumped to his feet when his name was called, and he met a doctor about his age at the plastic door. "I'm Walker Thompson."

"Tess is asking for you."

"So she's awake?"

"She took some heavy pain medication earlier today, got overheated, and was severely dehydrated. That's why she fainted."

"And her cancer?"

"We're running some tests, but she perked up once we got the IV in and regulated her body temperature. I can't speak about her cancer with what we've done so far."

Walker nodded and thanked the man, stepped past the curtain he indicated to find Tess propped up in a hospital bed. The air went right out of his lungs as if he'd been kicked in the chest.

He blinked and Tess's pixie cut morphed into Libby's luxurious curls. Curls that had turned limp near the end of her life. Curls Walker had thought of often in the first year after Libby's death. He hadn't imagined them for a while now and confusion made his stomach squeeze.

"Hey," Tess said, breaking the spell that had fallen over Walker.

He moved toward her, apprehension consuming him. He didn't want to walk away from her, but he wasn't sure how he could weather the strong storms it would require to be with her. And he had Michael to think about too.

He sank into the chair next to her bed. "Feeling better?"

"A lot better." Her fingers knotted in the corner of the sheet and her eyes flitted around the room, landing on various items—the clock, the curtain, the IV machine.

"I'm glad." He clasped his hands and let them hang between his knees. He wanted to reach out and comfort her, but the older, wiser part of him wanted to protect himself. Needed to maintain distance.

"They're going to keep me overnight." She finally trained her eyes on his, and Walker marveled at the strength he found in her gaze. "You don't need to stay. I'll call Paige, and she'll go get Graham."

"He can stay at Megan's," Walker said. "I'll take him down to Paige in the morning. Or he can just stay with us, roam at the ranch. Michael knows where he can go and where he can't." He needed something to drink in order to get his next sentence out, but he had nothing. "Maybe Paige can come pick you up tomorrow."

She flinched like he'd slapped her, her head falling back against the pillow and her eyes blinking, blinking. "I—I'll ask her."

Walker hated the raw pain in her voice. Despised that he was the one who'd caused it. He exhaled and stood. "I'll keep Graham until you get back tomorrow. Let me know about the tests, okay?"

It took every ounce of strength Walker possessed to walk out of the room, leaving Tess behind in that hospital bed.

He held his head high, his emotions storming and his cowboy boots banging against the worn tile in the hospital. On his right, he spotted a piano, and he detoured that way.

He played every Sunday night, and this one should be no exception.

As he sat at the keys, the tension and frustration drained from him. His mother had insisted all of her children learn to play every hymn in the hymnal. After that, they could quit. Walker had never fought his mother about the piano lessons, and he actually enjoyed his time on the bench.

His first thought landed on Libby, and the song he'd played at their wedding. His fingers twitched, but they didn't play. He thought of Michael's favorite song—*Consider the Lilies of the Field*—but bypassed that too.

His favorite song floated through his mind. A popular tune, usually accompanied with the guitar, *The Man Who Could Not be Moved*, rose into the air, soothing Walker from the inside out.

CHAPTER 6

Tess stared at the spot where Walker had last been. Had he really just walked out? Was he really going to make the forty-five minute drive back to Brush Creek without her? Did she really have to sleep in this emergency room alone?

Fear struck her full in the chest, the same voltage as the day she'd first heard those two terrible words. *Breast cancer.*

She felt disconnected from her body, almost like she was floating above it. All the familiar and annoying smells that came with a hospital muted. Someone walked by with a doctor, and their mouths moved, but Tess heard no sound.

Then beautiful music from a piano infiltrated the numbness surrounding her. Tess seized onto it and let the tune wash over her, cleanse her. Without thinking and without wasting another moment, she leapt from the bed, annoyed when the plastic tube of her IV prevented her from moving too far.

She grabbed the metal IV stand and towed it with her, uncaring that she was wearing a hospital gown. It was secured everywhere, and everyone here wore one. She scanned the hallway for Walker, like maybe he'd be leaning there, his cowboy hat pulled low over his face as he agonized over what to do.

He wasn't. Tess continued toward the sound of the music, drawn to it by an otherworldly force. The piano sat against a wall in a small waiting room that was completely empty except for the musician.

Tess paused at the sight of tall, athletic, Walker sitting on the bench, his large hands moving over the keys with gentle strokes. She breathed because it was involuntary. She couldn't seem to make the pieces of Walker line up. How could he tame wild horses and produce such beautiful music? How could he walk out on her, only to come here and make something so lovely and worthwhile?

She closed her eyes and basked in the tonalities of the piano, sure she'd never been soothed so completely. Finally, the last notes were pressed and the sound from the piano strings faded into silence.

Tess opened her eyes. "That was wonderful," she breathed.

Walker startled and twisted toward her. "Tess." With the fluidity of a man half his size, he rose from the bench and swept her into his arms. "I'm sorry. I'll stay."

She let him hold her, because it felt right to be in his arms. And she needed his strength to stay on her feet. She didn't say it was okay, because it wasn't. She hugged him back and said, "Come back and let's talk."

He kept one arm securely around her as they walked

back to her corner of the emergency room. A nurse met her there, and said, "There you are. We've got a room on the second floor for you. Are you ready to go up?"

She nodded. A room would be better suited for a private chat, and Walker would surely have more than a folding chair to sit in.

"I won't know the room number until we get up there," the nurse said. "Climb on in, and we'll go." She glanced at Walker. "Since you two aren't related, you'll have to check in at the second floor reception desk. I would give her about twenty minutes." She smiled apologetically as Tess watched Walker's reaction.

He flashed the nurse a smile so quickly, Tess could barely catalogue it. When his attention returned to her, all the hard edges of Walker Thompson softened. "I'll call Paige. Make all the arrangements for the boys." He lifted his phone, pressed a kiss to Tess's forehead, and walked out. At least this time, Tess knew he'd come back.

———

WALKER DIDN'T SHOW up in twenty minutes. Or thirty. Tess let the IV work its magic and though her stomach growled, she managed to doze off. A sound outside of her dreams brought her back to consciousness, and she blinked open her eyes to see a guilty look traipse across Walker's face.

"Sorry," he said as he finished sliding a tray onto the rolling table that would extend over her bed.

"Is that...?"

"Chicken noodle soup," Walker said. "I know you like it, and I tried it in the cafeteria, and it's really good."

Tess straightened, and used the remote to sit the mattress up further. "I'm starving." She beamed at him. "You always seem to know what I'm thinking, or what I need."

He chuckled. "I just knew I was hungry, and I figured you might be too." He sank into the recliner beside her bed, a long exhalation escaping his mouth.

She reached for the spoon and stirred the delicious-smelling soup. Her mouth watered as she thought about the salty broth and the chewy noodles. But she couldn't put a bite in her mouth quite yet.

"Look," she said. "I think I have a pretty good idea of why you left earlier." She looked right into his dark eyes, hoping he'd understand everything she didn't say. "But my cancer isn't back."

"Have you gotten the test results back?"

"Not yet." Desperation and frustration combined, creating an emotional cocktail that didn't sit well in Tess's veins. "So if I'm sick, you don't want to be with me, is that it?"

Walker's jaw twitched. He blinked. He studied her with a quiet stillness that unnerved her. Just when she thought he wasn't going to answer, he sighed. "I don't know," he said. "That sounds really bad when you say it like that."

"I don't know how else to say it."

"I'm not as strong as you are," he said, catching her by surprise. She gaped at him, the soup forgotten.

"What does that mean?"

"It means losing my wife nearly destroyed me, and I

don't know if I can handle losing someone else I care about."

A smile flickered across her face, but it didn't last long. She took a bite of soup, sure he had more to say and would need time to say it. Sure enough, by her third taste of the fantastic soup he'd brought her, Walker continued.

"And I have Michael to think about. If he...if I introduce another...." He shook his head, a nervous chuckle accompanying the movement. "This sounds stupid too. It's not like we're engaged or anything."

Tess's insides iced. Walker hadn't seemed like the type to date perpetually. But maybe that was what he'd do here. She wasn't sure when everything in her life had turned upside down. Or why she didn't really want to go home to Brush Creek without the possibility of having Walker by her side.

"No," she finally said. "We're not engaged."

"I'm scared," he said. "Because I really like you, and I think we could probably get to engaged pretty fast. But like I said, I'm not as strong as you are, and seeing you in that hospital bed really freaked me out."

Tess appreciated his honesty, also liked that the seemingly impenetrable Walker Thompson had fears and insecurities. It made him more human. More attractive.

She finished her soup in silence, one more question weighing on her mind. She leaned back, feeling better than she had in days. Feeling brave. "So now what?" she asked.

Walker took off his hat and scrubbed his hands through his hair. Thick, dark hair Tess would like to run her own fingers through. Her face heated and she nearly coughed, finally able to tear her eyes from Walker.

He said, "I don't know, Tess, but I learned something when I left you earlier."

"Oh yeah?"

"I don't like the idea of not being with you."

Happiness exploded through her, settling into excitement when he reached over and threaded his fingers through hers. "So maybe we can just see how things go? What do you think of that? You might get sick of me in a couple of days." He punctuated his statement with a smile Tess felt all the way to the bottom of her stomach.

"I doubt I'll get sick of you in a couple of days." Tess laughed. "I've put up with you for four years already."

"Oh, wow." He laughed, the sound bouncing around the tiny hospital room. "Put up with me, huh?"

She squeezed his hand, relishing in the sound of his laughter and the warmth from his skin. Her mind flew to thoughts of kissing him, and everything inside her tightened. She imagined his strong hands on her back, or maybe cradling her face, as his lips touched hers. Fireworks popped in her mind with the fantasy, and suddenly every breath was filled with the masculine smell of Walker.

She fanned herself with her free hand, prompting Walker to ask, "Are you okay? Is it hot in here?"

She dropped her hand to the bed. "No," she managed to gurgle. "I'm fine."

But, oh, she wasn't fine. She was in so much trouble if the mere thought of a kiss with Walker had her this wound up.

————

A week later, Tess bumped over the gravel lane in front of Walker's cabin, just like the previous Sunday. She'd sat next to him in church, endured a twenty-minute discussion with Alison and Paige in the shade on the sidewalk, and then taken a two-hour nap. She'd promised Walker she'd take care of herself; get the rest she needed; eat enough; drink enough water; all of the above.

And she had. She wanted to "see how things could go" with Walker too. Wanted it more than anything else she'd wanted since the death of her husband.

They hadn't been able to enjoy the chocolate cheesecake she'd made, and she'd instructed Walker how to wrap it in plastic wrap and then tin foil so it could be frozen. She turned off the ignition, Graham already running across the lawn toward Michael and the dogs.

Bruce and Wayne ran in circles around Graham, and then the older of the two—Bruce, the yellow lab—trotted over to Tess and nosed her thigh.

"Hey, boy." She scratched the dog behind the ears, crouching low so he could lick her chin. She laughed and pulled back, the slobber a little more than she was anticipating.

"Come on, Bruce," Walker called, and the dog immediately turned and ran back to the porch, where Walker stood with his hands stuffed in his shorts pockets, leaning against the post. She couldn't read his expression across the distance and under the cover of the shade, but his magnetism drew her feet toward him.

Wild ideas of stepping right up to him and pressing her lips to his ran through her head. She entertained them, just like she had all week. She wanted to let go of her inhibitions, the way she'd let go of everything in her previous life. She hadn't been able to grab onto her old life anyway, and she'd left Salt Lake City behind because of it.

And now, with Walker grinning at her, she wanted to do it again—leave behind who she was without him and find out who she could become with him.

CHAPTER 7

Walker was sure the gorgeous woman walking toward him was a mirage. Sure she was there to see someone else, maybe Justin in the next cabin down. He seemed to have plenty of female admirers.

Tess arrived in front of him, and he focused on her instead of the other cowboys at the ranch. "Hey," he said. "You look fantastic." He slipped his hand around her waist and drew her close. His lips brushed across her brow, and his eyes closed in a moment of bliss. He couldn't believe how easy it was to touch her, to kiss her, even if the real mark he wanted lay a few more inches south of where his lips had touched.

"Thanks," she whispered.

"Cheesecake's ready," he said, indicating the cabin behind him. He glanced out the yard and called to Michael.

He paused at the front gate, Graham and the two dogs right behind him. "Can we go over to the pool?"

Walker shook his head before his son had stopped

asking. Landon hadn't said anything about a pool party for that night.

He'd missed last week's because of the trip to the hospital, but the boys had really enjoyed themselves. Landon had a soft spot for dogs, and apparently everyone had gotten in the pool, human and canine alike.

"Dad, Landon said we could." Michael marched back over to him. "Bruce is dripping with sweat. He wants to swim."

Walker glanced down at Michael's swimming trunks. He hadn't even noticed when his son had changed, worried as he was about Tess's arrival. "I think *you* want to swim."

"Can you just text Landon?"

Walker whipped his phone from his back pocket. "When did you talk to him?"

"This morning after church, while you were—"

Walker whistled so Michael would stop talking. He cut a glance in Tess's direction, noting the open curiosity on her face, before focusing on a text to Landon. He didn't need her knowing he'd watched her for a good fifteen minutes while she chatted with her friends. He hadn't been close enough to hear, but he could read lips well enough, and he knew the shape of his name on Tess's lips.

He wanted to know a lot more about Tess's lips. He cleared his throat like she could hear his thoughts and finished his text. To give himself more room to think—room without her intoxicating floral perfume—he stepped back.

Landon's text came back in the affirmative. "You were right." He nodded to Michael. "Grab some towels and the sunscreen first. You listen to Landon and Megan. Be respectful."

Michael whooped and dodged back into the house. With the boys and the dogs gone, Walker had nowhere to focus his energy but on Tess.

"So it's just you and me for cheesecake."

She ducked her head, her left hand reaching up to tuck her hair behind her ear. It was so short, it didn't stay, but the gesture indicated that she'd had long hair at one point in the past. She'd had the pixie cut for as long as he'd known her.

"This cheesecake is going to blow your mind," she said.

"I'm counting on it." Walker opened his cabin door and waited for her to walk through it.

———

A COUPLE OF WEEKS LATER, Walker's patience hung at the end of a very short rope. He'd spent a couple more evenings with Tess. One sitting across from each other at Crusiers, the diner where everyone hung out on the weekends. One side-by-side at the movie theater, their sons sitting in the row in front of them. They'd sat beside each other at church. Held hands whenever they were together.

But he hadn't kissed her yet. And he knew she wouldn't be the first to make that move. For some reason, he hadn't been able to either. He had been scared about her cancer returning and the impact that would have on him emotionally, as well as Michael. But he'd spent time outside, away from the cabin, early in the morning before work. And he'd found peace about dating Tess.

Now he just needed to gather his wits, find his courage, and kiss the woman.

"Time for school!" he called up the stairs. Michael should've been down ten minutes ago. He'd have to eat breakfast on the go. Walker picked up the new backpack they'd bought the previous weekend as Michael came thundering down the steps.

"Dad, I can't find my shoes."

"Your shoes?" Walker felt stitched together wrong. Michael seemed so old, starting fifth grade. It felt like a milestone, and Walker generally struggled with the milestones of Michael's life, because Libby didn't get to experience them.

He glanced around. "The shoes we bought two days ago? Didn't you wear them over to Landon's last night?"

"No, I wore my skate shoes."

"Did you take—?"

"Here they are." Michael dove under the kitchen table and pulled out the blue athletic shoes. He jammed them on his feet and Walker draped him in the backpack.

"Let's go. We have to stop and get Graham too." Walker hustled Michael out to the truck and he drove faster down to town than he ever had. He had to get the boys to school on time and get back to Brush Creek to work with a new horse that Landon had bought last week.

Magnolia was a real firecracker, and she'd been giving Walker a run for his money. Still, he loved the tall, leggy, Appaloosa. She'd make a fantastic barrel racing horse, and Walker was determined to make her the best the rodeo circuit had seen in decades.

He pulled up to Tess's house and found her and

Graham standing on the front porch. He hadn't anticipated seeing her; she'd said she liked to sleep in. But she walked toward him, not a hair out of place, with makeup on her face, and a bounce in her step. He rolled down the window and she leaned her elbows against the truck.

"So Michael will come home with Graham. You'll be down around six?"

"Yep." He let the movement from the two boys distract him. "Six. Michael has the money and the signup form for the soccer in his backpack."

She grinned and tapped his truck as she stepped back. "Sounds great."

"Hey," he said as she continued to back away. "I heard you cut hair in your basement."

"You heard?" She cocked her eyebrows and laughed. "You've known that for years."

His fingers wandered to the back of his neck. "Wondering if you could cut mine tonight."

The rosiness in her cheeks vanished and her hand fluttered around her throat. "Sure, I guess," she said with a heavy dose of doubt.

He gave her a wide grin. "Great. See you at six."

———

Walker arrived back at Brush Creek along with a heavy gust of wind. He pressed his hat to his head and hurried past the shed and bunk house toward the indoor horse arena. Justin, a lanky cowboy with bright blue eyes and a loud laugh that always made Walker smile, lounged on the top rung of the fence. Inside the circle, Landon rotated with the horse, a male Quarter Horse who'd come to them from California. He was originally being trained to be a team roping horse, but he bucked too much. Landon wanted to train him according to his strengths, make him into the greatest gelding the rodeo had seen in the bronc riding category.

"He's big," Walker said as he leaned on the fence next to where Justin sat.

"There you are."

Walker's defenses came up. "Had to drive Michael to school."

"Megan was looking for you."

Walker kept his face blank, his eyes on the brown horse trotting around the arena, one eye on the plastic bag Landon kept tapping on the ground, and one navigating himself around the oval.

"How's Bear doing?" Walker asked, ignoring Justin's statement completely. He'd catch up with Megan later, probably at lunchtime. He'd like to keep his sanity for the next three hours, thank you very much.

"Saddle," Landon called, and Walker hustled away to get the equipment. He lost himself to saddling, and brushing down, and training horses. He enjoyed the quiet, steady work. The way his muscles tightened and released. The way the air tasted clear and crisp out here in the Utah wilderness.

By the time he finished with Magnolia, the mare he was trying to get to trust him completely, the arena and barns were empty. Walker dusted his hands together and headed toward Landon's house. The pool glinted in the sunlight, almost blinding Walker, and he glanced around the backyard where he'd enjoyed many summer barbecues. He tapped on the glass of the backdoor and then opened it.

Landon stood at the kitchen counter, spreading mayo on a piece of bread. "How's it going with Magnolia?"

"She's comin' along," Walker said. "I think she'll be ready in a couple of weeks. Then Ted will start her with the barrels." He stepped to the sink and started washing his hands.

"Sandwiches." Landon nodded toward the spread. "We're eatin' out front."

Megan had set up the front patio area with what she called "the cowboy pad," and the boys ate there most days. Walker put together a turkey and ham sandwich, and had taken three steps toward the front door when Megan appeared in the mouthway of the hall.

"Not so fast, Mister."

Walker didn't try to conceal his groan. "I'm starving, Megan."

"Talk fast then."

"Talk about what?"

She folded her arms. "Tess Wagner."

"Nothing to talk about."

Megan scoffed. "Right. You've been sitting by her in church. Driving down to town in the evenings."

"So what?"

"Are you dating?"

"You could say that."

A wide grin split Megan's face, and she squealed as she closed the distance between them. "It's about time, Walker." She hugged him, nearly smashing the sandwich between them. Walker held it out to the side and awkwardly patted Megan on the back.

She stepped away, and he said, "I don't really know what I'm doing."

"You'll figure it out. Dating is like riding a horse."

Walker chuckled, the sound without much humor. "Well, that's not true. Riding a horse is a lot easier."

"Says you." She cast him a look over her shoulder and went into the kitchen to clean up the meat and cheese.

Walker escaped to the patio, hoping to calm his churning stomach with food.

Chapter 8

Tess finished her only haircut for the day by eleven and then paced in the kitchen for an hour until she finally pulled a pan out of the cupboard and practically cracked her stovetop when she dropped it onto the burner. She set another pot a little more carefully onto another burner and flipped on the hot water.

She went through the motions of making her mother's macaroni and cheese recipe. She didn't have to think. She didn't have to measure. Her hands just moved, completed tasks, and half an hour later, she had a steaming pan full of ooey gooey mac and cheese.

Her stomach revolted at the thought of eating it, but she served herself a bowlful anyway. She stared at it, her thoughts finally catching up to her actions.

"There is no way," she muttered to herself. Having Walker in her tiny hair studio was not going to go well. Touching his scalp so intimately? With his intoxicating scent filling the air from floor to ceiling?

No way she could survive such a close encounter without kissing him. She took a bite of the mac and cheese, glad she didn't need conscious thought to create something so creamy and delicious. Maybe she should just kiss him when he showed up. Get it out of the way.

They'd been spending more time together, but he hadn't made a move farther than holding her hand and draping his arm around her shoulders. Her lips tingled in anticipation. She would definitely be kissing Walker before she went to bed that night.

"He's going to be in the house." Sudden fear seized her though he'd been there a few weeks ago, after the apricot festival. She pulled out the air freshener and the vacuum, did the dishes, and had both bathrooms sparkling by the time the boys burst through the front door, laughing and pushing each other.

"Hey!" She tossed the paper towel she'd been using to clean the mirror into the trashcan. "How was the first day of school?" She drew Graham into a hug, surprised when Michael joined them. "Third grade and fifth grade. Must've been awesome." Her voice stalled in her throat as she hugged not just one son, but two.

Not her son, but a boy who needed a mother's touch.

"It was great," Graham said, pulling away and dumping his backpack in the middle of the floor. "My teacher is so funny. She told us this story about her son and her dog and they were so muddy!"

Tess nodded and "hmm"'ed in all the right places, but she kept her eye on Michael. He was polite and accepted the bowl of mac and cheese she gave him, and when Graham finally stopped talking, she said, "How was fifth grade, Michael?"

"Good. We had to take a lot of tests," he said, and that was all. She wondered if Walker would be able to draw more out of him, get him to say more, but Tess didn't quite know how. "Any homework?"

"Just papers my dad has to sign."

"Graham?"

"I have some notes too." Graham finished eating and headed toward his bedroom, calling for Michael to come with him.

"Clean up your bowl first," Tess said.

Michael got both dishes, slid Tess a smile, and disappeared down the hall with Graham. Though they'd just eaten, she knew they'd be hungry by six o'clock, when Walker was supposed to make an appearance. So she took the cookbook from the cupboard above the stove and started flipping through it, her thoughts running through what a cowboy would like to eat after a long day of breaking horses.

She'd just taken the meatloaf out of the oven when the roar of a truck's engine outside caught her attention. She strode to the back door. "Boys!" she called. "Time for dinner." Graham came tearing toward her from the swing set in the corner of the yard.

By the time the boys spilled into the house and Tess turned around, Walker filled the doorway. His broad shoulders distracted her, and Tess stumbled back into the kitchen.

"Something smells amazing." Walker's gaze followed her

and it felt like it weighed two tons as she stirred the mashed potatoes one final time and dropped in a slip of butter.

"Meatloaf and mashed potatoes," she said.

"Can't go wrong with that."

Graham slid onto the barstool where he normally sat to eat, and Michael joined him. "Do you like meatloaf, Michael?"

He glanced at his father, who nodded. "Yes, Miss Tess."

She grinned. "So polite." She filled two plates with food and said, "Let's say grace. Walker, do you want to say it?"

Color shot into his cheeks, but he nodded. She bowed her head, her heart tap dancing in her chest like it wanted to make as much noise as possible. Walker said a beautiful prayer about gratitude and he asked a blessing on her for her health, which touched her so much she didn't hear the rest of his sentiments until the boys said, "Amen."

Walker joined her in the kitchen and collected a plate. "It doesn't seem fair that you can cook *and* bake."

Her heart tripped at his near proximity, at the amount of food he piled onto his plate. She took her food to the table in the corner of the kitchen, which only housed two chairs. With just her and Graham, she had two of every-thing. Two barstools. Two chairs. Two bedrooms.

Two chances? she wondered. She'd fallen in love with her first husband after only a few dates. Dared she hope she could have another chance at having a partner in life?

"You've hardly eaten." Walker's voice cut through her thoughts.

"I ate a lot for lunch," she said.

Walker took her mostly full plate and took it with his

back into the kitchen. "I sent the boys over to the park. Should we go get them?"

She glanced around, just now noticing that the kids weren't there. Foolishness snaked through her. How catatonic had she gone? "What about your haircut?"

"We can do it after we grab the boys."

Tess swallowed. "All right. But just a sec."

Walker paused on his way to the front door, turning back to look at her. "Yeah?"

She moved toward him, and she must've had something on her face, because Walker backed up, a stern look on his face. "Oh, boy. Just a minute."

"Just a minute?" She leaned into him and put both of her hands on his chest.

"I didn't think you'd make the first move." A smile flirted with his lips. "But I have a plan, missy."

"A plan?" Confusion made her smile collapse. "A plan for what?"

He leaned close. Closer still. He was going to kiss her right now. Her eyes drifted closed. Right now. Any second now.

"A plan for kissin' you," he said, his breath drifting across her neck, his voice almost a growl. He stepped back and said, "So come on. We're going down the street to Oxbow."

With his absence, she nearly fell forward. He tucked her hand into his and asked her about her day as they went down the sidewalk. The park seemed full of families, couples, dogs running after Frisbees. Even though it was the first day of school, the sun would be up for hours still, and Tess enjoyed the fall evening breeze against her skin.

He didn't take her toward the playground area, and he strayed from the path in favor of walking closer to the stream she loved. He talked about a horse named Magnolia until Tess thought she'd go mad.

"When are you going to get to the plan?" she asked.

He stopped and chuckled. "Impatient little thing, aren't you?" He reached up and ran his fingers down the side of her face. "You're a beautiful woman, Tess."

She grinned and leaned into him. His hands slipped to the small of her back and tucked her against him. "I guess I don't need to ask if I can kiss you."

She shook her head and closed her eyes, the anticipation of kissing Walker only second to the actual moment when his lips touched hers. He moved passively, seeking permission. She gave it eagerly, and he finally kissed her like he meant it. Tess held on, drew it out, experienced Walker in a whole new way.

———

"COME IN!" Tess yelled, not that she needed to. Paige and Alison had already twisted the doorknob and were stepping through the house. Tess backed out of the fridge holding a tray of the most perfect chocolate mousse she'd ever made. "I hope you ladies brought your A-game."

Alison scoffed. "You think pudding can stand up to my chocolate soufflé?" She eyed the mousse like it had no business being at a chocolate party.

"This is *mousse*," Tess said. "It's so much more sophisticated than pudding."

"Doesn't matter," Paige said, sliding a cake stand

housing a gorgeous treat onto the counter. "None of it is going to stand up against my chocolate-chocolate chip cake with a candy bar topping and chocolate frosting." She swiped her finger across an edge of the cake. "Homemade."

Tess admitted defeat to herself, determined not to give in publicly until everything had been tasted. But Paige knew how to bake a cake up right, that was for sure. "Where's Shirley?"

"She can't come tonight. The bakery was getting a fresh shipment of fruit and she had to go in to get it all inventoried and prepped."

Tess reached for the silverware drawer. "All right then. Let's get tasting."

Paige swiped the spoons from her hand. "Oh, no. You have to tell us about Mister McDreamy Cowboy first."

Tess ducked her head. Her first kiss with Walker was only two days old, and he'd left thirty minutes ago, after they'd shared another spectacular kiss. She still had the taste of him in her mouth, and chocolate had suddenly become number two on her list of things she wanted to experience every day.

"He kissed me on Monday night."

"Finally," Paige said, sagging onto a barstool. "Was it wonderful?"

Tess sighed. "Spectacular."

"Let's try the cake." Paige moved around the counter and plucked a knife from the block next to the stove. She raised the knife to cut wedges, but Tess stopped her.

"You've forgotten the right way to cut a cake." She took the knife and cut the cake right in half, turned the cake and cut it in half again. Several more cuts across the cake and

Tess placed the knife in the sink. "See? Now there are four slices that are special. They have the most frosting. And, if Shirley were here, we'd each get one."

"You and your traditions." Alison shook her head, wearing a fond smile, and accepted her piece of cake. She took one bite and moaned so deep that Tess knew she'd never beat Paige's cake with a simple chocolate mousse.

CHAPTER 9

"Who cut your hair?" Landon asked the moment Walker walked in the barn the next morning.

He didn't see any reason to hide it. "Tess." Monday had held a lot of firsts for Walker, something he absolutely wasn't upset about.

"Looks nice." He went back to filling feed bags. "Things are going okay with her?"

"Just fine," Walker said, thinking fine was such a poor word for how things were going. He hadn't kissed a woman since Libby. Kissing Tess had reset his center, making him feel something he hadn't experienced in a very long time.

He didn't want to be alone anymore, something he'd never expected. When Libby had died, he thought all he'd ever need in his life was Michael. After all, every time he looked into his son's eyes, he saw Libby's.

But now he'd opened the door to other possibilities, and he'd walked all the way through. The grass wasn't greener, but it was new. Different. Exciting.

He realized he'd stopped working and was just standing in the middle of the barn. He ducked his head as Justin, Ted, and Emmett came around the corner. He lifted his hand in a wave, but he didn't want to talk to them. No, today, he wanted to be inside his own head, working with an animal that listened but didn't offer advice.

As he clucked his tongue at Magnolia, got her to walk in a circle and step over the stick, and finally come to him in the center of the ring, his thoughts didn't stray to Tess.

But to Libby.

By evening, he was physically and mentally exhausted and he still needed to drive down to Tess's to get Michael. He wanted to see Tess and he didn't at the same time. When he knocked on the door, he waited for her to answer.

She pulled open the door and leaned into it, her beauty striking him like lightning in the chest. "Evenin' ma'am."

She giggled. "Shut up."

"Is Michael ready?"

"You don't want to come in?"

Walker suddenly did. "I suppose I can come in for a few minutes." He stepped into her house, glad when she didn't move back to give him room. He did what came naturally to him—he wrapped one arm around her and pulled her in for a kiss.

Everything aligned inside Walker. "It's good to see you," he murmured, his lips catching against hers.

"Dad?"

Walker looked over Tess's shoulder to see Michael standing there, his hazel eyes—his mother's eyes—wide and shocked.

"Hey, bud. How was school?"

"Are you—?" He swallowed and looked at Tess, who'd twisted toward him but hadn't put a single inch between herself and Walker.

"Are you guys dating?" His gaze volleyed back and forth between Walker and Tess.

A cold stone settled in Walker's stomach. He should've spoken to Michael about this new relationship with Tess. The boy was nine now, would be ten by the end of the year. Of course he knew what dating was.

He exchanged a look with Tess and stepped past her. "Michael."

"Are you?"

Walker had always appreciated when his parents had been honest with him. A stab of guilt reminded him of how long it had been since he'd spoken with them.

"Yes," Walker said. "Tess and I are dating." He crouched down and put one hand on his son's shoulder. "You don't like that?"

Michael shook his head. "I don't know. I—I just—"

Walker waited for him to continue, employing every ounce of patience he had. "I should've told you. Talked to you about it."

Michael stooped to get his backpack. "Let's just go."

"Michael." Walker straightened as his son marched out the front door. He exhaled and brushed his fingers along Tess's as he passed her. "I'll call you later."

She nodded, a brave mask cemented in place. Walker wanted to stay and comfort her, but he kept his feet moving in the direction of his son.

———

WALKER DIDN'T TURN to head back up the canyon to the cabin. Michael kept his gaze out the passenger window, his chin supported in his hand.

"You want some of those fried cheese curds for dinner?" Walker asked, unsure of how to have this conversation. He tightened his fingers against the steering wheel and offered up a plea for help.

"I guess," Michael said.

Inspiration didn't strike him, so Walker kept the truck moving toward the next small town, Beaverton. A dive of a diner served garlic burgers and fried pickles and shakes made with hard ice cream. Walker had discovered the place on his way into town five years ago, and he'd gone back often, usually when he needed an escape from Brush Creek.

He loved both towns, but less people knew who he was in Beaverton, and Walker needed the anonymity sometimes. Like tonight, when he needed to have a hard conversation with his son.

He pulled into the parking lot, the dusky sky around them reminding him of how much he just wanted to kick back and relax with a steaming cup of coffee. He pushed down his frustration and exhaustion.

"Michael, I'm sorry."

His son finally looked at him, and the hurt in his hazel eyes sliced right through Walker.

"You like Miss Tess, don't you?"

"Yeah, sure, she's nice." Michael switched his gaze out the front windshield. "She hugs me after school. It's...nice."

Walker's heart expanded two sizes. Megan had been right. Michael needed a motherly touch in his life. Guilt and gratitude pulled through him at the same time, making the idea of eating anything unappealing.

"That's great," he said, his voice on the choked side. "Sometimes grown-ups...well, our relationships evolve." He stopped. Did Michael even know what evolve meant? "They change. I've been friends with Tess for years. We've been doing that cotton candy fundraiser for a while. And this summer...." He didn't know how to articulate his feelings in an appropriate way for a child.

"You decided you like her," Michael said. "Like you like-*like* her."

Relief washed through Walker. "Right. So we started, um, hanging out more, and holding hands. Normal stuff adults do when they like-*like* each other." He cleared his throat. "Stuff you shouldn't do until you're older. A lot older."

Michael gazed back at him steadily. "So will Graham and I be brothers?"

A chuckle burst from Walker's mouth. "Oh, son, I just started dating Tess. It could go nowhere." He swallowed. He definitely wanted their relationship to go *some*where. "Or we could date for a long time and then get married. But it's not going to happen anytime soon." He didn't want to admit to his son—or himself—that he was going slow on purpose, searching for the right thing to do, exploring all the possibilities, examining all the ramifications of a relationship with Tess.

He extended his hand toward Michael, who scooted across the seat and allowed Walker to hug him. "I love you, bud. You'll always come first."

Michael hugged him back, making Walker realize that

he didn't hug his son as often as he should. Everything had become about finding the shoes, and eating breakfast so they could go, and getting to work on time.

Tess had been taking care of the after-school things. She'd signed the boys up for soccer, had snacks waiting for them at the house, the whole nine yards.

As he climbed out of the truck and waited for Michael to follow him, Walker realized that he needed to be more than a dad who signed the papers and found the shoes. He wanted to be a counselor for his son, a friend, *and* a father. He felt inadequate to be any of the three, but he pasted on a smile and hooked his arm around Michael's shoulders.

"You gonna try the grilled cheese challenge?" He grinned at Michael, who grinned right back.

"Gross, no."

Walker tipped his head back and laughed, and not only because he agreed. A hamburger should not be sandwiched between two grilled cheese sandwiches. It wasn't American. They ordered, and with plates of burgers and fried food in front of them, Walker finally felt like he'd settled things with his son.

In his back pocket, his phone buzzed, and he ignored it. It would be Landon or Tess, and he wasn't prepared to talk to either of them yet.

CHAPTER 10

"I just think we should be smart." Walker's hushed words didn't soothe Tess. She'd put Graham to bed an hour ago, then eaten more cake than any one person should in a single day. Finally, Walker had called, but now she didn't like what he was saying.

She didn't know how to be smart when it came to Walker. They'd known each other for years. She understood his loss on a personal level—better than almost anyone. Both of them had lost spouses in an accident, and a bond existed there she'd always felt. She just hadn't realized she could have him be her best friend *and* her boyfriend.

"So I'm taking Graham strawberry picking this weekend," she said, unsure of how to address his *smart* comment. "Do you and Michael want to come?" The fall strawberry picking was a tradition she'd established when she'd moved to Brush Creek. She'd always gone alone with Graham; she'd never even invited Paige or her family, or Alison, or anyone.

"I always come back and make fresh strawberries and

cream. We can have a little picnic in my backyard. Or yours. Or at Oxbow."

Walker remained silent so long she thought she'd lost the connection. She checked her phone right as he said. "Sure, Tess. That sounds nice."

She wasn't sure what *nice* meant either, and she hated how she was now analyzing every word the man said. Her head pounded, and it wasn't only because of the sugar over-load. "Great," she said. "I'll see you in the morning."

"Listen," he said. "Don't be mad, all right?"

"I'm not mad."

"I mean about tomorrow, when I don't come all the way to the door to get Michael. It really has nothing to do with you. I just want him…. He needs to know I care about him as much as I care about you."

Warmth filled the icy spaces in Tess's soul. "All right." They hung up, and Tess floated upstairs to her bedroom. The next evening when Walker tipped his hat to her from the driver's seat instead of leaning in her doorway with a sexy smile etched on his face, it did hurt. She did feel a flicker of anger, a tiny flame of resentment. Michael hadn't acted any differently. He'd accepted her hug, the container of applesauce and the cheese stick. He'd run down the street with a fishing pole in his hand, Graham hot on his heels as they went over to Oxbow Park to catch crawdads.

She hadn't made dinner, and though she hadn't done much of anything else that day, she felt bone-weary. She wondered for a few brief moments as Walker's truck disap-peared around the corner if she should go see her doctor in Evanston. She'd felt better after the hospital stay in Vernal, and she'd kept her promise to Walker. She was taking care of herself.

But something still wasn't right.

Something non-physical gnawed at her too. With this new distance between her and Walker and a considerable cooling in their relationship, she wondered if he really needed to know everything right now.

"Mom, I need help with this." The frustrated sound of Graham's voice drew Tess away from the front door, where she still stood. She closed the door and joined him at the kitchen counter, where he had a worksheet in front of him.

She tousled his blond hair and smiled into his dark eyes. Her husband had been blond and light-eyed, but somehow, Graham had almost chocolate-brown eyes. With a start, she realized what was eating at her.

She and Walker would never have a child. She would never be able to look into her son or daughter's eyes and see Walker's. Or find the familiar shape of his nose, or the midnight quality of his hair. And he would never be able to do that either.

"What have you got?" she asked Graham in a voice barely above a whisper. As she helped her son figure out two-digit addition, the loss of something she didn't even know she wanted dug at her.

She'd always been satisfied with just having Graham. She'd never fantasized of having a whole houseful of children, though with the sale of the scrap metal salvage, she certainly had enough money to stay home and take care of them.

While Graham ate a bowl of cereal for dinner, Tess escaped to the backyard and dialed Walker. She hung up before the first ring finished. He wouldn't be able to comfort her in this right now. He hadn't even spoken to her today.

Helplessness threaded through her, stitching every breath tighter tighter tighter. She'd felt like this in the days and weeks following Brandon's death, and she was well acquainted with fear, and grief, and desperation.

Tess took a deep breath and calmed herself. She sank onto a chair and watched as the sun inched lower and lower through the sky. A constant prayer ran through her mind as she searched for a solution to the things that troubled her.

When the last of the light left the sky, she stood. She didn't have a definitive answer, but the same one the Lord had always provided for her. *One day at a time.*

So she went inside and started helping Graham get ready for bed. They'd made it through another day, and tomorrow would bring new possibilities.

———

AFTER GRAHAM WENT TO SCHOOL, Tess called her doctor in Evanston and scheduled an appointment for the following day. For some reason, she didn't want to tell Walker about it. The boys had soccer practice after school anyway, so she dialed Paige.

"Hey, I need a favor," Tess started. "I have to go up to Evanston tomorrow. Could you take Graham and Michael to soccer practice? I should be back by six for sure, to meet Walker."

"Of course," Paige said. "They can walk home with Linus."

"Great." Tess smiled to herself as she puttered around the house, putting away a tea towel and then wiping down the already clean counter.

"Are you feeling all right?"

Tess bit her lip and tossed the washcloth into the sink. "Something's off," she admitted. "I'm just going to get some tests done, do another scan. Just to be sure." She swallowed hard against the lump in her throat. Having a relapse while she was dating Walker definitely wouldn't be smart. She could see him running for the canyon and never coming back down. Bitterness coated her tongue at the unfairness of life.

"When are you leaving?" Paige asked.

"As soon as Graham goes to school."

"Let's go to lunch today."

"Sounds great. Amigo Taco?" She loved tacos, and today seemed like the perfect day to splurge on her dietary choices.

Paige laughed. "I can't believe we have to drive fifteen minutes to get tacos."

"They're the best. And Beaverton isn't that far."

"Ten minutes then."

"They're *tacos*."

"Oh, that reminds me. I got you a new peanut butter to try." Something banged on Paige's end of the line. "I'll bring it with me."

A rush of affection for her friend made Tess smile. "Sounds great. See you in a bit."

A couple of hours later, Paige brandished a jar at Tess when she opened the door. "This is going to blow your mind."

"It's not peanut." Tess took the jar and twisted off the lid. "It smells fantastic."

"Cashews," Paige said, following Tess into the kitchen. "I read about it online. Supposed to be killer with strawberry-rhubarb jam."

"And I have some of that because your mom makes it every year." Tess set the jar on the counter and turned to embrace her friend. "Thank you, Paige." She held onto her tightly, hoping to convey how much their friendship meant to her.

"What's wrong?" Paige asked. She pulled back, kept a grip on Tess's shoulders, and peered into her face.

Tess's eyes watered, but she brushed at the tears. "Everything will be fine."

"But it's not right now. Tell me all about it." She hooked her arm through Tess's and gently led her out to her waiting sedan.

Tess didn't know where to start. She didn't have anything conclusive to go on with her cancer, so she decided to start with Walker.

———

BY THE TIME she arrived in Evanston, Tess's muscles needed to stand, stretch, move. Something inside her seethed, and she knew exactly what it was. She should've told Walker about her health concerns. She should've called her parents. They'd pray for her, alert her sisters, put her name on a community prayer roll. Walker would probably make sure to be there to pick up the boys after school, have dinner ready for her when she returned, all of it.

Or maybe that was her imagination running wild. But perhaps Walker would be waiting at her house with a platter of tacos as high as the Rocky Mountains. Just because he wanted to be smart about their relationship didn't mean he wanted to end it. Or even slow it down.

She pulled out her phone to make a few calls and realized she was five minutes late. She fired off a fast text to her mother as she hurried into the oncology building. She could call Walker afterward. She missed the sound of his voice, the steadiness he'd introduced into her life with the simple act of holding her hand and texting her before he went to bed.

A blast of air conditioning hit her as hard as the realization that she'd started to fall for Walker Thompson. She needed to call him now.

"Tess." The receptionist hurried toward her, a broad smile on her face.

"Nancy." Tess melted into the older woman's embrace and breathed in the familiar scent of roses and powder.

She held her at arm's length. "How are you feeling?"

"Good, good."

Nancy pursed her lips. "Why are you here then?"

"I just had a feeling I should come," Tess said. "And I've learned not to ignore those feelings." She stepped with Nancy to the check-in desk and leaned against it. Her phone felt like a brick in her pocket, but she ignored it when it buzzed. It would be her mother, and Tess couldn't talk right now.

"He's ready for you," Nancy clicked a couple of times on the computer and glanced toward the nurse standing there with a thick folder in his hand. "Good to see you again, Tess." She gave her such a fond look, Tess was reminded of how many people influenced her life. She'd tried to distance herself all these years—a mistake she realized.

"I need to call my mom first," Tess said. "Is that okay? She called right when I stepped through the door."

"No problem." Nancy nodded at the nurse, who smiled and went back down the hall.

She hurried outside and dialed her mom back. "Honey."

Tess's emotion lodged in her throat. "Mom."

"You're at the oncologist again? I thought your scans from a few months ago were clear."

Though the sun beat down on the cement, a chill snaked down Tess's spine. "They were. I've just been feeling a little bit off."

"You're smart to go in."

"I'm already late, but I just wanted to talk to you for a minute."

"How's Graham?"

"He's fine. I didn't tell him I was coming today."

Her mother sighed, and Tess imagined her mother's blonde hair piled into a messy bun on top of her head. It was just after eleven o'clock, which meant her mom had probably already completed her morning workout. She'd be wearing her yoga pants and tank top in either bright purple, teal, or yellow—her mother's favorite colors. Her bright blue eyes would harbor concern, and her voice held love as she said, "Of course you didn't."

"I didn't want to worry him. He's seven. He shouldn't have to deal with grown-up things."

"I'm glad you called me. I'll tell your father and I'm sure Mindy and Jami will want to know."

"Thanks, Mom."

A half a beat of silence sounded. "What else is bothering you?"

Even though Tess was a mother, she wasn't sure how her mom knew about more than Tess had said, especially over a phone line. She supposed she would pick up the skill with every year she spent with Graham, and she'd come to the doctor today so she could ensure she had as long as possible with him.

"I started seeing someone," Tess said.

"No...." The shock in her mother's voice made Tess laugh.

"Is it that hard to believe?"

"Honestly, Tess, yes. You left Salt Lake in order to—"

Tess knew what her mother was going to say. The argument was old, and no matter how many times it was discussed, their points of view had never aligned. "In order to have my own life," Tess said. "It had nothing to do with running away, with hiding from myself, with living alone forever."

Her mom cleared her throat. "So who is he?"

"He's the foreman at a horse ranch here in Brush Creek. His name's Walker Thompson."

"Walker Thompson."

Tess liked the way her mother rolled his name around in her mouth. "I have to go, Mom. I'll talk to you later."

"Call me tonight. I want to know what the doctor says and more about this Walker."

Tess smiled into the sunshine, a measure of peace

infusing her soul. She hadn't really been living her life alone in Brush Creek. She had friends, confidantes, her son. But she hadn't exactly made it easy for her parents to be involved with any of that. Hadn't really let anyone in past her core group of ladies. She didn't even hang out with the other moms when she took Graham to the park, and she didn't feel bad about it.

Though she was late, she took a few precious seconds to send a text to Walker. *Missing you today. Want to grab pizza and eat at my place tonight?*

Then she wouldn't have to cook. Not that she was using Walker to solve her dietary needs. She wanted to see him too. Tell him about her appointment and how she was feeling. Find out where he was emotionally.

He didn't answer, and she turned around to attend her appointment. After all, she couldn't keep the doctor waiting all day just so she could see if her boyfriend would bring her dinner.

Her mind tripped over the word *boyfriend*, but she grasped onto it and held it close. Maybe she was old-school. Maybe she was just old. But in her earlier dating days, if she was only seeing one man, holding only his hand, and dreaming about kissing him, he was her boyfriend.

Walker definitely fell into that category, and Tess was very happy about that.

CHAPTER 11

Walker arrived at Tess's house a few minutes before six. Her car sat in the driveway; the breeze rustled the leaves on the two birch trees in her front yard. Somewhere nearby, a dog barked. The whole scene seemed idyllic, and Walker wondered what he'd been worried about. Was he being smart or simply practicing self-preservation?

He'd felt himself going all-in with Tess, and it scared him. Had he used Michael to regain some distance, get the time he needed to figure out how he felt? Maybe.

Definitely, he thought, and a healthy dose of shame flowed through him.

He reached for the pizzas he'd picked up and left his negative thoughts in his truck in favor of eating and spending time with the people he wanted to be with.

The front door opened before his foot had touched the first step, and Tess appeared. She met him at the top of the stairs and took a deep breath. "Mmm. C'mon in."

He followed her, every nerve in his body firing on extra

cylinders. He wasn't sure what he'd been so afraid of. A petite, blonde woman?

He realized as he pushed the door closed with his boot that he was actually afraid of *losing* the petite, blonde woman. And if he never had her, he didn't have to lose her.

"I got one cheese and one combination," he said. "I don't know what Graham likes, but Michael is pretty picky about toppings."

"Cheese is perfect." She moved to the back door and called for the boys to come in.

Graham appeared first and he scanned Walker. "Did you bring your dogs?"

"No, sir," Walker said, throwing a smile at the boy as his face fell. "I will next time."

Michael appeared, and Walker set the pizza boxes on the kitchen counter and gave his son a hug. "Hey, how was school?"

"Okay," Michael said, squirming way from Walker. "Soccer practice was awesome. I'm going to play midfielder, because the coach says I'm a great runner."

Walker smiled at the pride in his son's voice and said, "That's great, Michael. Your mom—" He cut himself off as if he'd just used a horrible M-word. He blinked and looked at Tess before finishing with, "Your mom ran track in college. She was a great runner."

No one seemed to care that he'd brought up Libby. And they shouldn't. Walker had just never dated after her death, and he had no idea how to navigate this rocky ground.

Michael's head seemed to swell four sizes as he sat on

the barstool next to Graham. Walker should tell him more about his mother, as it wasn't only Walker who'd lost her.

"What are you playing?" he asked Graham.

"Defender." He didn't seem too happy about it, but Tess distracted him with food and soda.

Walker picked up a paper plate and handed it to Michael. He could get his own food and pour his own soda. The hint was taken, and Walker picked up three slices of combination pizza and grabbed a can of cola. Michael copied him, taking another slice of cheese pizza and snatching a lemonade before resuming his seat at the bar.

"We're eating on the picnic table," Tess said, heading toward the back door. Walker expected the boys to follow them, but they didn't. He set his food on the table and caught Tess before she sat down.

"It's good to see you," he said, keeping his voice low. "I liked your text today." He smiled at her and leaned down. She received his kiss with eagerness, in his opinion, and he took his time exploring her lips, tasting her mouth.

"Mmm." He finally forced himself to pull away, and she tucked herself against his chest.

"I texted you from Evanston," she said, setting all of Walker's internal alarms to wailing.

He thought he did a pretty good job maintaining his composure, especially when he asked, "Oh, yeah?" in a normal tone.

"I went and had all my tests done again." She shifted out of his embrace and sat at the picnic table. She waited until he positioned himself across from her, but eating was the farthest thing from his mind.

"I've been feeling a little off," she said. "So I thought I'd go in."

"What did you find out?"

"I'll know by Monday." She picked up her slice of pizza. "I wanted to talk to you about something else too."

"All right."

"Are you going to eat?"

"Are you going to start talking now?"

She smiled at him, but the gesture felt shy and fearful. "Have you thought about having more kids?"

Walker startled. Sure, he knew Tess. They'd been friends for years. But they'd only been dating for a short time, and most of the major life discussions hadn't crossed the table yet. He picked up a piece of pizza and took a big bite. He chewed as he tried to figure out the answer she wanted to hear.

In the end, he gave the answer from his heart. "Yeah, sure," he said. "I like kids, and I wouldn't mind having more." Whether she was ready to hear that or not, and whether Walker was ready to admit it, he began imagining what their daughter would look like. He'd seen pictures of Tess's first husband, and he was blonde and blue-eyed like her. What would a child with his DNA and Tess's look like?

She nodded, a wobble in her chin. "I can't have kids," she said point-blank. "I don't have the right parts anymore."

Walker abandoned his food and rounded the table. He slid onto the bench next to her and wrapped his arm around her shoulders. "It's not a deal-breaker."

She tilted her head back and gazed at him, her gray-blue eyes stormy yet hopeful at the same time. "It's not?"

"Tess." He traced his thumb over her cheekbone. "If we're meant to be together, things will work out."

She nodded. "Sometimes I hate how much faith it takes just to make it through the day." She laughed quietly, but it held more bitterness than happiness. "Would it be so hard to just let us know what will happen?"

Walker squeezed her. "I hear you, beautiful." He gazed into the distance, his feelings mirroring hers. "I hear you."

———

OVER THE COURSE of the next month, Walker thought a lot about what Tess had told him. Her tests had all come back clear, and that made him sleep easier. Not being able to have more kids didn't bother him as much as he'd originally thought it would. He had Michael, and she had Graham, and they could be a family together just fine.

No, what needled at his mind was her statement about faith. It did require a lot of effort to live each day in the right way. He wasn't sure if he should hold her hand more or less. Which was smarter? Kiss her longer or let her go? Talk to Michael again or wait for him to bring up the topic?

Walker didn't know about any of it. He wanted to be smart with the relationship, because he wasn't interested in losing his heart to Tess only to have it shattered. And he wouldn't do anything that would harm Michael.

He'd prayed to know what was right, but God had been pretty off-hands about the whole thing. He'd taken to playing the piano every evening after picking up Michael. He sang the lyrics he knew and lost himself in the music if he didn't.

One morning in the middle of October, he woke with the song Homeward Bound in his mind. He couldn't shake it during his shower, and even after he'd had two cups of coffee, the tune lingered in his mind. The wind howled outside his window, and he knew if he ignored the song in his mind, it would haunt him all day.

So after waking Michael and putting him in the shower, Walker sat at the piano and began to play the song he'd last played at his wife's funeral. He hadn't played it in five years, but his fingers knew exactly where to land, and the lyrics flowed through his throat with ease.

"In the quiet misty morning, when the moon has gone to bed...."

He finished the song and found Michael leaning against the piano. Walker hadn't seen him arrive, and their eyes met. "That was your mom's favorite song," he said. "I played it at her funeral."

"What does it mean?"

Walker sighed and lowered the cover over the piano keys. He leaned his elbows on the hard surface. "It means we have to trust that God knows what He's doing. He calls some people home, and allows others to stay. He has a plan, and we have to have enough faith to follow that plan."

Michael nodded like he understood. Walker barely understood. Sure, the words sounded pretty, and deep down, he knew they were true. But actually living them was much harder than just saying them.

"Dad?" Michael shuffled his feet, and Walker blinked to focus his vision.

"Yeah?"

Tears filled his son's eyes, causing Walker's heart to collapse on itself. "What's wrong, bud?"

He sniffled and let his big alligator tears drip from his chin. "I got in trouble at school," he blurted. "I need you to come meet with my teacher this morning, or I can't go to school."

Shock zipped through Walker with the speed and heat of lightning. "What happened?"

"It wasn't my fault, but Miss Triplehorn said she still needs to talk to you."

"Why didn't she call?"

Michael shrugged. "She said she would."

"You still haven't told me what happened." Walker leaned away from the piano and folded his arms, trying to figure out how to handle this situation. Michael had never gotten in trouble at school before. He'd started kindergarten in Brush Creek, and had been at the same school ever since. He'd never gotten a bad report card, and he was bright and helpful. At least all of his other teachers had said so.

"I hit a boy," Michael mumbled.

Walker's stomach plummeted to his boots. "Like, with your fist?" His eyebrows rose, as did the pitch of his voice.

"Sort of."

"How do you 'sort of' hit someone?"

"He said my mom died because she didn't want to be around me." Michael raised his chin and stared defiantly into Walker's face.

Walker forgot how to breathe. "He said that? Michael, you know that's not true, right? Mom was in a car accident. She loved you."

"I know." Michael's beautiful eyes shone like sunlight off still water. "When I said that, he shoved me. I—I." He swallowed. "Miss Triplehorn just wants to talk to you." He sniffed and wiped his face. "Can we go?"

Walker rose from the piano bench and gathered his son into a tight embrace. "Sure, bud. Let's go." His stomach writhed on the way down the canyon, squirmed at the gorgeous sight of Tess leaned up against the column of her house, tightened as his cowboy boots met the tile inside the elementary school doors.

"Go on outside," he told the boys, and he adjusted his cowboy hat as he ducked into the front office.

"Can I help you?" The secretary in front of him half-rose from her seat. "Oh, hello, Walker."

"Judy." She sang soprano in the church choir, and she'd tried unsuccessfully to get Walker to join. Her husband was a co-owner at the hardware store, and Walker knew Jim well. "I guess I'm supposed to meet with Miss Triplehorn this morning."

"Let me call down to her room."

Walker turned away from the front desk, and Judy said a few seconds later, "You can go on down. She's in two-oh-four. Third door on the right."

He raised his hand in thanks and made the walk down the hall, his heart thumping as loudly as his boots. He poked his head into the appointed classroom and found a tall brunette moving from one group of desks to another, dropping notecards on each one.

"Mornin'," Walker said, swiping his hat off his head.

The teacher turned toward him, her face breaking into a smile when she saw him. "You must be Mister Thompson."

"I am. Michael said I had to come in this morning." He wanted to give Miss Triplehorn the benefit of the doubt. If his son had been hit, he'd want action taken, even if Michael had done the taunting.

He moved into the classroom and Miss Triplehorn closed the door behind him. "Did Michael tell you what happened?"

"A nine-year-old version of it." Walker settled into the chair she indicated. "I'd like to hear your side."

She sighed as she sat next to her desk. "Michael is a sweet boy. I've never had a problem with him. I don't think he hit the other boy maliciously. I was told he was being taunted and got so upset that he started swinging." She folded her hands in her lap. "Of course, that's still not okay, as I explained to Michael."

"Of course not," Walker agreed. "I've spoken to him about it."

"I wanted you to know, and I need to be able to tell the other parents that action has been taken."

"I understand."

"Have you noticed any changes in Michael? Is he going through some changes at home?"

Walker's throat turned dry, and he barely scraped "I haven't noticed anything." But he knew at least one thing had changed: He'd started dating Tess. Sourness turned his stomach, but he managed to shake Miss Triplehorn's hand and hold his head high as he exited the school.

Once in the safety of his truck, he let his head sag to his chest. He thought of the song he'd played that morning.

When the summer's ceased its gleaming, when the corn is past its prime,

When adventure's lost its meaning, I'll be homeward bound in time.

It was definitely fall, and the corn had all come down weeks ago. He knew the song wasn't about ending a relationship with a woman, but about passing to the other side. Still, it spoke to him. He believed that he would be reunited with the people he loved—including Tess—at the right moment in time.

Maybe now simply wasn't the right time for them to be dating. He'd told Michael he'd put him first, and here he sat, stewing over what to do about Tess.

He pulled his phone from his pocket and dialed her. She answered with a fun, flirty tone, and Walker wanted to end the call. "Can I come over?" he asked instead.

"Sure," she said, her voice full of surprise. "Do you want to go to breakfast or something?"

"No, I just need to talk to you for a few minutes before I head back up to the ranch."

"All right. See you in a few."

Walker drove the several blocks back to Tess's, a nest of live snakes writhing in his stomach, his lungs, his throat. Tess waited on her front steps, her knees drawn to her chest. He fumbled getting out of the truck, a numbness spreading from the top of his head to the bottom of his feet.

He paused a healthy distance from her, sure he'd lose his resolve if he got close enough to breathe in the scent of her hair, feel the softness of her skin, look into the depths of her beautiful eyes.

"Tess," he said, his voice completely agonized.

She stood, her fingers fluttering around her collarbone.

She said nothing, making him work for what he needed to say.

"Michael's gotten into some trouble at school," he said. "I need...." He wanted to say *you. I need you*, but instead he said, "I need to focus on him for a while." He swept his hat off his head and ran his free hand through his hair. Everything in his life felt disheveled, like there'd been an earthquake and had shaken everything up.

"What does that mean?"

"It means I'll be picking him up from school. I can still take Graham in the mornings if you need me to."

"I can take him." Her words barely had any form at all.

"I'm sorry, Tess."

"Are you saying we can't be together?"

He shook his head. "I'm saying that I need to focus on Michael right now." He took a step toward her and then fell back. "Maybe we can just push pause."

She sucked in a breath. "I don't think so, Walker. It's either stop or go. There's no pause."

Walker's muscles tensed. "Then I guess this is stop." He mashed his hat back onto his head and turned away. "Sorry, Tess." He walked back to his truck, his step sure but his heart cracking, then breaking, then shattering. He drove away and managed to make it around the corner before slamming his palm against the steering wheel.

CHAPTER 12

Tess didn't see Walker again until the following Thursday, when he pulled up to her house and sat in his idling truck. Megan had called and asked if Michael could still come home with Graham for the last few weeks of soccer. *Megan.* Like Tess and Walker weren't grown-ups and couldn't have an adult conversation about something as simple as soccer practice. His behavior angered her almost as much as it tore at her heart.

He sat in his truck, his eyes straight forward, everything about him testifying that he had turned into a statue. Tess positioned herself next to the column on her front porch and folded her arms. She'd called upstairs to Michael, and now they all waited for the boy to gather his belongings.

He finally burst through the front door. "Thanks, Miss Tess," he called as he jogged past her.

"No problem, Michael. See you later." She lifted her hand in a wave, but the little boy didn't turn back. And Walker certainly wasn't looking. Tess tore her eyes from him and went back into the house. She would not be the one to show how much his absence sliced at her.

With the door closed, she pressed her back into it and took a deep breath. The thought of dinner overwhelmed her, and she wondered how far she could drive on the gas she had in her tank. Then she and Graham could stop wherever they happened to be and find a taco joint.

With a jolt, she remembered that Paige had invited her to dinner that night. She flew into action, grabbing her purse and snatching her keys from the drawer by the garage entrance. "Graham!" she called. "We're going over to Paige's for dinner. Let's go."

Footsteps pounded upstairs and then flew down to the first floor. "I haven't finished my homework."

"That's okay," Tess said. "We can do it in the morning before school." She tried to give him her best smile, but it felt stitched on. "Grab your shoes. You can put them on in the car."

So though Graham needed a bath, and still wore his soccer practice clothes, and hadn't finished his homework, Tess took him over to her friend's house.

Paige had a pair of boys, one thirteen and one nine. Graham immediately glued himself to Scott's side, leaving Tess alone with Paige and her husband Bryan.

"How's life?" Paige asked as she chopped cucumbers. Chop, chop, chop. The knife scraped as she collected the pieces and dropped them on top of the lettuce.

"Fine."

Paige paused, her hand hanging in midair as she reached for a tomato. "What happened?"

Tess shrugged. How she'd managed to avoid Paige for

almost a week was a complete mystery. Sometimes their lives intersected every day, and sometimes they didn't.

"Walker Thompson broke up with her," Bryan said in a bored tone, not even bothering to look up from his tablet.

Horror snaked through Tess's bloodstream. "How did you know that?"

"Yeah." Paige drew the word out and narrowed her eyes at her husband, who finally felt the weight of it and looked up. "How did you know that?"

"He came into the hardware store today, lookin' miserable—about like her." He nodded toward Tess. "I overheard him talking to Jim about it. I guess he'd ordered something for...something with Tess, and now he didn't need it."

Tess felt like someone had scrubbed out her insides with steel wool, and then poured bleach down her throat. She covered her mouth with one hand, sure she was going to be sick. But she kept breathing, kept blinking, kept smelling the deliciousness of the beef roast Paige had obviously put in the crock pot hours ago.

"When did this happen?" Paige asked.

"Last Friday."

Understanding crossed her friend's face, and a sympathetic tilt appeared on her lips. "I'm surprised you came tonight."

Tess shrugged though she felt like every movement might crack a bone. "I was living before Walker. I'll survive." How she'd do that, she wasn't exactly sure, but she'd made it through the past six days. Sure, she'd cried a little over the weekend. She'd skipped church so no one would see her puffy eyes, and Graham accepted her declaration of "I'm sick," and left her alone.

And maybe she'd eaten all the ice cream she could find at the convenience store on the north end of town. She went there, because she knew Walker wouldn't. At least three other gas stations existed between the ranch and the northern edge of town, and she didn't want him to see her in sweat pants, as many of those pint containers as she could carry in her arms.

And maybe, just maybe, she'd had a chocolate party of her own last night. Wednesdays were made for desserts, and she didn't see a reason to waste one just because the ladies weren't coming over.

"Oh, honey." Paige wrapped Tess in a tight hug. "There's more to life than surviving."

"Not for me," Tess mumbled into her friend's shoulder.

Paige stepped back like she'd been electrocuted. "What does that mean?"

"It means I've spent the last five years of my life surviving. First when Brandon died. Then when I was diagnosed with cancer." A rage Tess didn't know how to calm rose within her. "You realize that's what you do when you have cancer, right? You survive. There's no cure." Sharp edges tore at her lungs. Coming over here was a mistake. She shouldn't be around people when she felt so ragged.

"I was just starting to think I could live, and maybe with Walker, and then...." She shook her head as tears filled her eyes. "It's fine. He needs to take care of Michael, and if there's anyone who understands that their kid comes first, it's me." She glanced around like one of Paige's famous chocolate cakes would materialize on the counter in front of her. She'd probably start fisting it in at this point. "It's not like I was in love with him."

Paige's eyebrows rose right up to her hairline. "No?"

"Of course not." Tess added a hearty scoff to her statement. "We'd been dating for what? Two months? If that."

Bryan, who Tess had always liked, said, "Paige and I were engaged after two months."

"That's because we're crazy," Paige said quickly. She gave Bryan a look that clearly said *not helping. Be quiet.*

Bryan shrugged and went back to his tablet. Tess didn't mind what he'd said. Everything was different when you were twenty-something, single without kids, still in college. Their dating experience compared to hers was like trying to make an apple taste like an orange.

Paige snatched the tomato and cored it like it had done her a personal wrong. "Well, Walker's an idiot then. And here I thought you guys were perfect for each other. You've been friends for so long, and have so much in common." *Slice, slice, slice.* She made fast work of the tomato and continued her tirade as if she were alone in the kitchen. "How does a reasonable man miss what's standing right in front of him? I'm so going to give him a piece of my mind next time I see him." Her dark hair swished with every syllable.

Before Tess could beg her not to say anything to Walker, Paige strode to the mouth of the kitchen and called, "Boys! Time for dinner." She turned back to Tess, her stern expression melting into compassion. "Come on, honey." She draped one arm around Tess's shoulders and whispered, "I made a chocolate cake, and you can have two pieces."

Tess smiled even as emotion choked in her throat and

tears filled her eyes. Even if she never had another chance at marital happiness, she'd always have Paige.

———

A WEEK LATER, the barbs that had taken up permanent residence in her heart had dulled. She could get up without thinking about Walker. Drop Graham off without looking for Walker's truck. Enjoy Taco Tuesday without thinking about the teasing sparkle in Walker's eyes or hearing his deep voice teasing her about how no one needed to eat one hundred tacos.

She helped Graham's class decorate marshmallow spiders at their Halloween party; soccer season ended; the first snow appeared in the Uinta Mountains. Tess survived it all.

She went to church really late every week so she could sit somewhere far from Walker. She couldn't risk accidentally getting a whiff of his cologne or even catching a glimpse of his handsome face. And if she sat far enough behind him, she didn't have to see or smell anything that would make the sharp points inside her return.

Just over three weeks after Walker put a stop to their relationship, Tess laid in bed, keeping her promise to herself to take care of herself. Her fingers traveled around her chest, feeling for what she hoped never to find again.

She sucked in a breath and went back.

She stared at the ceiling. It couldn't be.

But it was.

Another lump.

Chapter 13

"When are you gonna stop moping around?" Landon sank into the chair opposite Walker, they being the only two on the front patio that day. Walker had sent Ted and Justin down to Vernal for more feed, and Emmett hadn't come in from the hay fields yet.

Walker bit into his peanut butter and banana sandwich and glared. He swallowed, said, "I'm not moping."

Landon gestured between the two of them. "What do you call this then?"

Walker looked at his plate, still half-covered with potato chips. "Eating lunch."

Landon rolled his eyes. "I know what moping looks like, Walker."

"Have I been slacking on the job?"

"No, of course not." Landon stuffed half his sandwich in his mouth, but Walker knew that wouldn't deter him from saying what he wanted to say. At least he chewed and swallowed first. "Has Michael had any more problems at school?"

Walker narrowed his eyes. "No."

"So you could maybe push play again."

"Landon."

"Walker, you're *unhappy*. I've never seen you as happy as you were when you were dating Tess."

Walker hadn't been that happy in years. He'd admitted it to himself in the quiet moments before he went to sleep. He'd thought many times about getting to Tess as fast as he could, apologizing for everything from what he'd said to global warming, and begging her to take him back.

He'd managed to make it through five weeks without doing that. He'd spent the time with his horses and his son, and he knew that world. Had once thought that world was all he needed.

"What's keepin' you from going back to her?" Landon asked.

"Pride," Walker answered immediately. "And fear."

"You think she won't take you back?"

"I don't know what she'll do."

"You think you can't be happy with her?"

"Of course I could be happy with her."

Landon finished his lunch. "I don't know what you're doing then."

"Living in fear, not by faith." Megan had appeared in the doorway.

"Hey, sunshine." Landon stood and pressed a kiss to Megan's cheek. He disappeared into the house and Megan took his place at the table across from Walker.

"Megan," Walker warned. "I just heard it all from Landon."

"Just tell me if I'm right."

Walker's heart stormed in his chest. "About right," he clipped out between stiff lips.

Megan smiled at him, a soft, kind smile that reminded Walker that she cared about him. "Fear gets you nowhere."

"Sometimes faith doesn't either," he said.

"It only seems like that."

"Yeah, well." Walker pushed himself up and gathered his now-empty plate. "Thanks for lunch, Megan." He cleaned up in the kitchen and went back to the horse barn. The work was never-ending, and for once, Walker was grateful for that.

That evening, as he stirred the spaghetti he'd just dropped into boiling water, Michael entered the kitchen. "Dad?"

"Yeah?" He glanced over his shoulder to find Michael carrying his backpack.

"I have to do a science fair project, and I need help picking an experiment."

Walker groaned. He hated school projects, because he usually did more work than Michael. "When's it due?"

"Next week."

Walker abandoned the stove. "Next week? Have you been workin' on it in class?"

"A little. I just need help finding a project."

"How could you work on a project if you haven't picked one yet?"

"I had a good one," Michael said. "But someone else got it approved before me."

Walker didn't much care what had happened. He just wanted to get dinner over with so he could go to bed. Now that the sun set sooner, Walker's limit came earlier as well. "Let's get out the laptop."

Michael followed him into the living room. "Dad, why did you stop dating Tess?"

Walker froze, his hand halfway in the drawer where he kept the computer when he wasn't using it, which was most of the time. "I told you," he said. "Wasn't a good time."

"You liked her though, right?"

"Yeah, sure, I liked her." Walker's voice sounded like he'd swallowed glass.

"How do you know when it's the right time?"

Walker pulled out the computer and faced his son. "I don't know, Michael. I honestly don't."

"Well, I liked her too." Michael sat down on the couch and unzipped his backpack. Walker stared at him for a moment, unsure as to what the conversation meant. Probably nothing. Over the course of the next couple of hours, he managed to feed Michael and himself, and then settle on a science fair project that would determine how much sugar was in different types of sodas. Michael would be able to boil them down himself, weigh the remains, most of it.

Walker went to bed only a few minutes after he'd tucked in Michael, and he spent a few extra minutes in meditation. *How do I let go of my fear?* he thought.

Walker didn't get an answer from the Lord, because he already knew the answer. He needed to have faith, just like the song he'd played at Libby's funeral.

Bind me not to the pasture. Chain me not to the plow.

Set me free to find my calling and I'll return to you somehow.

He turned his thoughts to Libby, and asked her, "What should I do?"

She didn't answer either, and though she'd passed away years ago, Walker still knew her as deeply as he knew himself. And if she were still alive, she'd do exactly what Megan had already counseled Walker to do.

Swallow his pride and get on over to Tess's.

It took him another week to make such a big swallow. Plus he had to wait for the cookie butter to arrive. It finally did, and he smeared the biscoff spread on one piece of bread and added a healthy amount of apricot jam—Tess's favorite —to the other side.

With the sandwich as a peace offering, he drove down the canyon to drop Michael off at school. Part of him wanted to scamper back up to the ranch, eat the sandwich for breakfast, and figure out how to live without Tess Wagner. The other part pleaded with him to get on over to Tess's and tell her how he really felt.

He turned right instead of left, then another right, and then he arrived at Tess's house. Her car sat covered in snow, untouched. Was Graham sick? Was Tess? Why hadn't she cleaned off the car to take him to school?

Walker approached the front porch with apprehension, a swarm of angry ants crawling through his blood. He almost smashed the sandwich into a single layer, and he coached himself to ease up on the bread. He noticed the walk hadn't been cleared; everything in Tess's yard was unmarred by footprints.

His first thought was that she'd moved. But her car sat in the driveway. The big snowfall had been the previous morning, and it had been gray and cold ever since. So she hadn't left in twenty-four hours. Didn't mean anything.

He knocked on the door, his heart beating as fast as hummingbird wings. Graham answered the door in his pajamas. A grin split his face. "Hey, Walker."

"Who is it?" Tess appeared and pulled the door open a little further. "Oh." She fell back and tugged at her sweater as the scent of something sweet and rotten filtered out of the house. "Hello."

"Are you okay?" He tried to peer past them to see into the house, but the interior was too dark to see much. "Do you need me to take Graham to school?"

She put one arm around him protectively. "He's not going today."

"No?" He scanned the boy. "Are you sick?"

"No, my mom—"

"Graham, go see what Grandma is whipping up for breakfast." Tess practically spun him out of the doorway.

Walker's curiosity meter went all the way to high. "Your mother is in town?" He'd never known Tess to have visitors, least of all her family.

"She's here to take care of Graham." Tess lifted her chin but didn't offer any additional explanation.

"I brought you a peanut butter sandwich." He brandished the concoction toward her. "It's not peanut butter, obviously. But I think this would make a killer last meal."

He expected her to smile, to welcome him into her

home, kiss him and say all was forgiven. Instead, she blinked. Blinked faster. Tears fell.

"Tess." Forgetting about the sandwich, Walker stepped into her personal space and wrapped her in his embrace. Every cell in his body sang to be holding her again, relieved she'd let him. "It's just a sandwich."

"I've been eating one everyday," she said, her voice barely her own. "See, I found another lump, and they're saying I need to have a mastectomy."

Walker's blood turned to ice. It moved through his veins with the speed of a glacier, and it hurt. "A mastectomy?"

"On Thursday."

Three days. No wonder her mom was in town.

"I'll go with you," Walker said.

She shook her head and opened her mouth to say something, but Walker blurted, "Tess, please. I'm so sorry. I'm miserable without you, and I want to go again."

She searched his face, her eyes bright and hopeful. "Even though I'm sick?"

"Especially because you're sick. That's what you do when you love someone. In sickness and in health, you know?"

"Love someone?" Her words hung like ghosts in the air.

"Yeah." Walker shivered and it could've been from the cold. "I love you, Tess. I was stupid, and I was hoping you'd take the sandwich and tell me you loved me too, and somehow get over how stupid I was."

Several beats of silence passed before she said, "You were just trying to take care of Michael."

"That's what I told myself too." He nodded a couple of

times. "But I was just scared. I still am. But I'm more scared of *not* being with you. So here I am."

A slow smile spread across her face. "Here you are."

He lifted the sandwich toward her again. One corner of it had smashed inside the bag. "You really should try this. It's life-changing."

She took the plastic bag. "Well, I would like my life to change." She retreated into the house. "Come on in. I hope you're ready to meet my mother."

Walker wasn't sure about anything, but he followed her into the house, infusing faith into every footstep.

"Mom." Tess paused on the edge of the carpet that delineated the kitchen from the living room. Walker sidled up to her side just as her mother turned. "This is Walker Thompson, the man I've been telling you about."

Walker rather liked the sound of that, and his fingers fumbled over Tess's until they aligned, matched, clasped together.

Her mother, also a blonde, turned from the stove, where the smell of hot butter tickled Walker's nose. "Walker? Oh." Understanding lit her blue eyes, and Walker squeezed Tess's hand.

"That's my mother, Marjorie." Tess gripped Walker's hand like she needed his anchor to stay standing.

"Ma'am. Nice to meet you." He stepped forward and shook hands with the older woman who'd clearly given Tess her blonde hair and blue eyes.

"Likewise." She shot a glance filled with a dozen questions at Tess. "These sandwiches are ready."

Graham cheered and said, "I want the one with hazelnut spread."

Walker's palette rebelled. He couldn't think of a single breakfast sandwich that should include hazelnut spread.

"Then hazelnut spread you shall have." Marjorie beamed at Graham like he was a heavenly vision and scooped what looked like a grilled cheese sandwich out of the pan and onto a plate.

"What's goin' on?" he whispered to Tess, both eyes still on the not-so-breakfast sandwich as Marjorie cut it in half diagonally and served it to Graham.

"We decided to make grilled peanut butter sandwiches," she said. "That one has hazelnut spread and strawberry jam."

Walker's eyes darted to hers. "Your last meal?"

She gazed at him with such affection, such…love that Walker sincerely begged the Lord not to take her from him so soon. Right there in her kitchen, the prayer ran through his mind, his heart, his very soul.

"Hopefully not today." A glimmer of a smile touched her lips just before she stretched up and touched her mouth to his. The kiss lasted only a moment—they were in mixed company after all—before she said, "Which one would you like?" She moved around him and glanced in the pan. "Mom has a regular old peanut butter and banana sandwich, and I know you like those. I thought honey almond butter with peach preserves sounded good." She lifted the zipper bag holding the cookie butter sandwich he'd brought her.

"You can have either one. I'm going to eat this." The grin she gave him this time held enough wattage to light the room, and Walker basked in the warmth of it.

"I guess I'll take the peach one," he said, though he

thought they all sounded pretty unappetizing. But for Tess, he'd experiment with any combination of butter and jelly until her dying day.

And though he'd vocalized his love for her just a few minutes ago, Walker realized the strength and truth of the statement in that very moment. Tess hadn't said it back, but he'd felt her emotion in the brief kiss, seen it in her eyes. She loved him too, even if she didn't know it yet.

———

"Okay, so here's his backpack. He doesn't usually have homework on Thursdays, because he has tests on Fridays." Walker glanced around like he was forgetting something. He was, he knew it. He just didn't know what it was.

Ever since he'd gone to Tess's on Monday morning, Walker's life had spun completely out of control. He'd barely worked with the horses, instead relying on Ted and Justin to pick up his slack as he made plans to travel to Evanston with Tess.

"Walker," Megan said. "It'll be fine. Your house is literally across the street." She stood with one hand on Michael's shoulder, both of them facing him.

"He's eaten breakfast," Walker said weakly. He hadn't eaten, and the tremors in his legs testified of it. "He's ready for school. You can help him boil down the sodas tonight?" He looked at Michael. "They're in the fridge at the cabin. You do what Landon and Megan tell you. Take good notes. I can help you with the display board when I get back."

"Got it, Dad." Michael stepped into Walker and gave him a hug.

"It's going to be fine," Walker whispered to him. "You have the phone I got you? I'll call you tonight." He crouched down and looked into his son's eyes. "All right?"

Michael nodded. "All right."

Walker straightened and patted his back pocket. Wallet, check. His coat pocket held his keys. A duffle bag already waited in the truck for the three nights he'd be staying near the hospital, near Tess. He supposed anything he'd forgotten, he could buy in Evanston. And anything Michael needed could be found at the cabin or in town.

Megan drew him into a crushing hug, and said, "Go on, now, cowboy. Go take care of your girl."

Emotion choked in Walker's throat, especially when Landon embraced him too, clapping a couple of times on his back and stepping away. The two men locked eyes, and Landon nodded, his throat working as he swallowed.

Walker turned and left before he couldn't make himself go. Before his friends and his son saw him lose his cool. He sat in his truck for a few seconds, his eyes pressed closed, and his head bent.

"Lord," he prayed out loud. "I know what I want. I've already asked you for it a hundred times. Now I'm just askin' for the faith and patience to handle whatever happens."

A sense of peace filled Walker's soul and he grasped onto it, carried it with him down the canyon to Tess's house.

———

NERVES ASSAULTED Walker on the long drive to Evanston, and not just because of the woman seated beside him, her thigh flush with his. They'd had easy conversation, avoided the topic of her surgery and cancer, and now silence prevailed.

"When are you going to go to the cemetery?" she asked, finally landing on one of the harder topics between them.

"I don't know. Later." Walker hadn't been to visit Libby's grave once since her death. He'd left Evanston completely to find a new life, and he'd never gone back. He'd confessed as much to Tess, and she'd suggested he take some time while he was in town to go to the gravesite.

"I have something else I want to talk to you about." He shifted in the driver's seat and cleared his throat. His mouth felt like someone had poured sand in it.

"What's that?"

"You have all your legal documents, right? Driver's license, that kind of stuff."

"Yeah." She turned and looked at him, the weight of her eyes heavy on the side of his face.

"We left early enough, and I was thinkin'...maybe we should stop by City Hall and get married before we go to the hospital."

The air in the cab turned still. Hushed. Reverent.

"Married?"

Walker lifted one shoulder in a shrug. "Yeah, I mean, I love you and you love me, and...I'll take care of Graham if anything happens to you." He cut her a glance. "Not that anything's going to happen, Tess. It's not. I just—"

"You think I love you?"

A grin climbed across his face. "I can feel it in the way

you kiss me. Remember how this isn't my first rodeo?" He chuckled and slid one hand off the steering wheel and into hers.

"It's not mine, either."

"Then you should know you love me."

"I don't need you to take care of Graham," she said in a meek voice. "My mom's already said she'd take him if anything happens to me."

"I know you don't *need* me to," he said. "But I know what kind of life you want to provide for Graham, and that ain't the life your mom has in Salt Lake."

"I'm not going to marry you just so you'll keep Graham in Brush Creek."

"I wouldn't expect you to." He squeezed her hand, the miles rolling under the tires before he employed his bravery and added, "You're gonna marry me because you're in love with me." He flicked his eyes to her and back to the road. Not another living soul drove on this expanse of highway, and he kept his gaze on her for longer the next time he looked.

"All right," she said in that pretty little twang of hers. "I'm in love with you, so I guess we can get married." She smiled for all she was worth, and Walker swung the truck onto the shoulder.

He smiled back at her and ran his fingertips down the side of her face. "I knew it," he whispered just before he kissed her like a man who'd fallen completely head over heels in love. Because he had.

CHAPTER 14

T ess smoothed down the blouse she wore. At least it was pink, one of her favorite colors. She'd never imagined she'd get married again, let alone wearing jeans and a cotton blouse. At the same time, the simplicity of it appealed to her. She did want Graham to stay in Brush Creek, and she did love Walker Thompson. She just hoped her mother—and Paige—would forgive her for getting married without them.

"Now or never," she whispered to her reflection, glad she'd decided to put makeup on that morning. They'd take it all off before the surgery, but since that wasn't scheduled until mid-afternoon, and Tess had the long drive to endure, she'd put herself together properly.

She took one last look into her own eyes and smiled at what she saw there. An abundance of happiness. An inkling of faith. An enormous amount of love. She smiled and shook her head. "I can't believe you fell in love with your best friend," she said to her reflection before turning and exiting the restroom.

Walker waited on a bench across the lobby, and he stood when he saw her. "You ready?"

He'd paid for the marriage license, and they'd put their names on the waiting list for City Hall. It seemed to be a slow Friday at the beginning of December to get married, so they'd only been waiting about twenty minutes.

"We're next," he added, taking her hand in his.

"I'm ready," she confirmed, lifting her chin. She was ready for it all. To marry Walker. To have the mastectomy. To come out the other side a survivor. To live her life.

A clerk opened the chapel doors and called, "Walker Thompson and Tess Wagner."

He looked at her, and she looked at him, and together, they took the first step toward their future.

Her pulse tried to pounce out of her chest as they passed row after row of empty benches, so unlike her first wedding. But everything in her quieted, all her concerns floated away, with the steady grip of Walker's hand in hers.

They arrived at the front of the hall, where a man wearing a black suit stood. He didn't look like a preacher, but he beamed at Walker and Tess.

"That's the mayor," Walker whispered. "He's an old friend of mine."

The man laughed. "An old friend of Libby's." The mayor stepped forward and drew both of them into a boisterous hug. A giggle escaped Tess's lips. "She'd be so happy you're getting married again."

"Okay, Terrance," Walker said, straightening his black-and-white plaid button-down shirt. Not exactly his finest, but Tess didn't mind so much. "We just need to get married and get on out of here."

"You always were so impatient." His smile seemed permanently stuck to his face, and his infectious personality testified to Tess of how he'd gotten elected.

"Do you often perform wedding ceremonies?" she asked.

He turned his blue-eyed gaze on her. "I happened to be walking by when this guy was applying. I can spare a few minutes." He stepped behind a pulpit and glanced down as he sobered slightly. "Did you want to call anyone? Have them on speaker for the ceremony?"

Tess glanced at Walker. "Maybe my mom?"

He pulled his phone out of his back pocket. "I'll call mine too."

After Tess had given the short run-down of what was happening, she had her mother and Graham on speaker phone, and Walker had his mother and father on the line too. He emitted a nervous chuckle and drew her back into his side.

"Okay?" he asked.

"Okay," she said.

"Okay!" Mayor Terrance boomed. "Dearly beloved, we have called you here today, to witness the union of Walker Thompson and Tess Wagner." He glanced down. "He is one lucky man to have found such a beautiful woman for a second time in his life."

Walker tensed and then chuckled. "Terrance, pretty sure that's not in the script."

The mayor laughed. "But you are lucky."

"And I know it," Walker said.

Tess liked the banter between them, and she sensed a friendship there that went deeper than she knew. She glanced up at Walker, a rush of love for him infecting her. She listened to the mayor get back to the script, and when she needed to, she indicated that yes, she'd love and cherish Walker in sickness and in health, for better or worse, for richer or poorer.

After Walker pledged the same vow to her, Terrance asked, "Anything to add?"

"I love you with all my heart," Walker said.

"Sorry," his mother said from the phone. "We didn't hear you."

"I love her with all my heart," Walker practically yelled toward the phone.

Laughter burst from Tess's mouth. She inched closer to the podium where the phones rested. "And I love you, Walker."

Faint sniffling came through her phone, the sounds of her mother crying.

"Well, then, I now pronounce you husband and wife." The mayor came around the front of the podium. "Go ahead and kiss your wife, Walker."

Walker leaned down, then hesitated. "Best wedding ever," he whispered just before kissing her so completely Tess had to hold onto him for dear life, which was exactly what she wanted to do everyday for as long as possible.

"That shipment of hazelnut and almond butters should be here tomorrow." Walker bent over a list in the kitchen of the cabin. "I've ordered two dozen loaves of bread from the bakery. I'll pick them up on Saturday morning." He glanced up at Tess, who sat on the barstool she'd brought from her house.

"And I'll be driving down to Vernal on Thursday to pick up the sugar, the cardboard tubes, and the plastic bags."

They'd had this conversation for years. Who was going to order what for their cotton candy booth, when things would arrive, what they should charge.

Walker's face had melted into a goofy smile Tess had seen him wear a lot over the past eight months. "What?" she teased. "Is my wig crooked?"

He blinked, chuckled, and leaned across the kitchen counter. "Your whole mouth is crooked," he whispered just before he kissed her. "But I kinda like it."

She held onto the sides of his face. "Do you think

selling the grilled peanut butter sandwiches at the festival is really a good idea?"

"Of course," he said, his dark eyes seeing right past all her fears, all her sorrows. "Who doesn't like something fried in butter?"

"You don't."

He drew back and smiled. "I don't like peanut butter in general. I'm not a good sample to draw from."

"You like that biscoff stuff." He'd ordered it by the case over the course of the last several months, and Tess had to admit it was delicious. He ate it on waffles, on crackers, on toast, sometimes right out of the jar. He would not eat it on fruit, she'd discovered. He'd labeled himself a "fruit purist," something she'd tried over the course of their short marriage to change, but Walker was steadfastly sticking to his guns on that one.

"That's because it's made from a cookie," he said, focusing on his list again. "Do you think we should donate to the National Widow and Widowers Foundation again, or do you want to give the money to the Breast Cancer Research Fund?" He glanced up at her, and he was the most magnificent man she'd ever met.

"Breast Cancer," she said. "If that's okay with you."

"It's fine with me." He checked something off on his list and came around the counter. "You want to go to Oxbow today?"

Though they'd shared the holidays together last year, and celebrated both Michael and Graham's birthdays, as well as each of their own, nothing quite held the magic of spending time with Walker at Oxbow Park.

"Yeah." She relaxed into his embrace. "Let's go to the

park for dinner. We can grab tacos before we go." She glanced at the clock. "And if I start right now, I can have a German chocolate cake ready in time."

He grinned and brought his mouth to hers in the sweetest kiss she could imagine. "I love you, Tess," he said, the edges of his lips catching against hers.

She adored him. She enjoyed living in the cabin at the horse ranch, and she loved that he'd been by her side every step of the way since the successful mastectomy last year. She kissed him with all the passion and love she had, and he growled. "Maybe you won't have time to make that cake." He swept her off the barstool and started down the hall.

"Walker." She giggled. "Where are Michael and Graham?"

"Landon got a new horse," he said, ducking into their bedroom. "They won't be back for hours." He kissed her again, deepening the connection between them.

"You won't have cake at the park if you do this," she whispered breathlessly.

"I have faith that you can do both." He grinned and gazed down at her with such love, a warmth spread through her entire body.

She giggled at his mention of faith. They'd had to take a lot of steps filled with faith in the past few months. First, the wedding, which Paige had pouted about for a solid month until coming around to forgiveness and acceptance of Walker.

She'd moved out of her house in town and in with him. It had been harder than she'd thought, but now she loved being out under the wide sky, closer to the mountains, farther from the gossip and happenings of town.

And her faith was stronger than ever. Even if she only got a little bit of time with Walker, she knew it would be worth the risk. He'd said so too.

"I love you, beautiful." He reached up and gently tugged on the edge of her dark wig to get the adhesive to release. "This'll be the first thing to come off."

She watched his face as he lovingly removed one of her many wigs. His eyes roamed her face; his fingers stroked over the little wisps of hair that had grown in since the chemotherapy treatments. "Feeling good today?"

She closed her eyes and nodded. "Real good today." Her scans had been clear for months. The mastectomy and follow-up treatments had worked their magic. For now, she was cancer-free. And she'd never been happier. "I love you, Walker," she whispered, and he captured her mouth with his again.

Read on for a sneak peek of the next book in the Brush Creek Cowboys series, **THE COWBOY'S CHALLENGE.**

Renee Martin stood on the fringes of the ice cream social, her eyes sweeping the church's multi-purpose room for her cousin. Of course, Leah stood with a group of mostly men, and Renee sighed. Leah would be no help tonight, and Renee straightened her shoulders.

She didn't need help mingling with the townspeople of Brush Creek. She wasn't even sure why she cared; she wasn't a permanent resident of the city. If it could even be called a city. With her, the population barely tipped nine thousand. Of course, Vernal wasn't much bigger. It only seemed that way because of all the tourists going to Dinosaur National Park, where Renee would be starting her new job the following week.

She needed an apartment in Vernal, but she hadn't been able to find one. Truth be told, she hadn't even looked. She pushed away the adult things she didn't want to deal with and focused on the long tables set up along one wall of the room. A bona fide ice cream bar. At least the pastor in Brush Creek knew how to bring people into the church.

A twinge of guilt cut through Renee, but she stuck that back down into her gut too. She liked ice cream. As she smoothed her palms over her shirt and felt the extra layers and curves she had, she knew it was pretty obvious to everyone that she liked a lot of ice cream.

Leah intercepted her before she could join the end of the line. "Come meet these guys." She glanced back over her shoulder to where the pod of males waited.

"Not interested," Renee said without letting her gaze linger on the men. If she did, she'd surely find one she found attractive, only to have Leah choose him as her next boyfriend. It had happened before, twice.

Leah laughed like Renee had just said the wittiest thing on the planet. Renee rolled her eyes and tossed her dark brown hair over her shoulder. "Leah, stop it. Have you already forgotten the disaster you created for me only two days ago?"

Leah sobered and blinked as if she had truly forgotten. "What? That thing with Justin Jackman?" She waved her hand like she was swatting away an annoying fly. "That was nothing. He's too uptight anyway."

Renee reached for a plastic bowl and handed it to Leah before taking one for herself. She'd thought Justin was cute, but she hadn't been properly informed of the situation before going in. She wouldn't make that mistake again.

"You should've mentioned that you'd dated him." She picked up a spoon and a napkin.

Leah scoffed. "It was barely four or five dates. I didn't think it mattered."

"Obviously, it did." Renee scooped several slices of banana into the bottom of her bowl. If there was anything better than a mint chocolate chip banana split, Renee didn't want to know about it. Her hips were already two sizes too big. "And I didn't think Justin was uptight."

That caught Leah's attention, and Renee's stomach twisted. Why hadn't she learned to keep her big mouth shut around Leah?

"Really? You liked Justin?" For some reason, her cousin thought it was her life's mission to find Renee a boyfriend. If Renee had been any good at doing so herself, she might have resisted harder. At least she'd had a few years at college without Leah's constant meddling—and Renee had dated exactly one man. The relationship hadn't gone anywhere, and they still kept up with each other online and through texts.

"I didn't *like* him," she said. "I just thought—"

"Renee, hello." The pastor stood in front of the ice cream tubs, beaming at her. "It's good to see you."

Renee smiled and said, "Hello, Pastor Peters. I'll have the mint chocolate chip."

He dug his scoop into the appointed tub and gave her two perfectly sculpted spheres of ice cream. Her mouth watered and she wondered if she could escape Leah so she could enjoy her treat instead of standing with a group of men, nibbling around the edge of the sundae while she pretended to dislike ice cream.

She'd just spooned hot fudge into her dish when Leah said, "Well, here's your second chance, Ren. Justin just walked in."

"Leah, don't you dare. I just want to eat my ice cream,

chat with a few ladies from the knitting club, and go home."

Leah laughed again, and Renee swore she added extra decibels just to get people to look. Thankfully, Justin wasn't one of them. But a couple of Leah's girlfriends must've known the laugh was the Bat Signal, because they swarmed.

"Hey, girls," Tawny, a tall leggy blonde, said. "Have you tried the mocha caramel crunch?" She took a bite and moaned. "It is to die for."

"Who looks interesting tonight?" Karla asked, glancing around. She carried a bowl of mostly melted ice cream, and her narrow waist testified of her self-control over the best treat on the planet. "There's a few guys here from Beaverton that look like they might be fun."

Renee tried to edge away, but Leah said, "Ladies, tonight is all about Renee," and her feet grew roots. She even forgot about her banana split though she still held the bowl.

Tawny squealed and turned in a full circle. "Who's the lucky guy?"

Renee's stomach fell all the way to the floor. "Leah, no."

"Justin Jackman." Leah slid her spoon into her mouth with a satisfied smile. "I dare you to go over there and ask him out."

"I am not doing that," Renee hissed. "I already made a fool of myself in front of him. He clearly wasn't interested."

"You didn't even try the other night."

"I did," Renee said, and she'd detailed everything she'd said to Justin. He wasn't uptight, like Leah claimed. He simply wasn't interested in Renee. He'd made that much clear, and though it had stung, Renee wasn't that broken up about it. Sure, he had thick, brown hair and blazing blue eyes that seemed to see more than just Renee's physical features. She'd liked that, but with only one real relationship under her belt, she was rusty on her small talk skills.

"It's a bet," Leah said, digging in her pocket and pulling out a twenty. "What have you girls got?"

Renee felt the ground slipping from beneath her feet. "Guys, no," she tried anyway. But in only seconds, the pile of cash in Leah's hand had reached a hundred dollars. She stared it, her mouth salivating in the same way it had over the mint chocolate chip ice cream. She'd graduated two weeks ago, jobless, with nowhere to go and nothing to do. She'd never wanted a career. Growing up, all Renee had ever wanted to do was get married and have children.

But she'd need more than a few dates for that to happen. So she'd moved in with Leah and done one adult thing: applied for jobs at the nearby National Parks. Utah had a lot of them, and Dinosaur had bitten. Thankfully, it was only a forty-five minute drive from Brush Creek.

Renee knew it was time to grow up and start taking care of things; become self-reliant. But just because she was twenty-four and a college graduate didn't mean she knew what to do with her life.

"One hundred fifteen dollars and twenty-one cents," Leah declared, and Renee's resolve died. She needed the money.

"Fine." She handed her bowl to Karla and ran her fingers through her hair. "What do I have to do?"

"Get a date with the hunky cowboy, and this is all yours." She flapped the bills in Renee's face. She made a swipe for it, though her cousin ran a couple of miles every day and could certainly take Renee before she reached the exit.

Renee straightened her blouse and fluffed her hair again. She located Justin standing with another cowboy who had a blonde-haired woman on his arm and two boys in front of them in line.

She could just pretend she hadn't gotten any ice cream yet. Adding confidence to her step, she strode toward the ice cream bar again. Justin didn't glance at her or turn toward her when she sidled up behind him.

Standing there, extreme awkwardness descended on her. Just when she was about to reach out and tap his shoulder, he twisted slightly toward her and retrieved something from his pocket. He glanced in her direction as a capsule of orange Tic Tacs made an appearance.

Her dang saliva glands were really having a workout. She'd grown up eating orange Tic Tacs like they were candy, not breath fresheners.

"Hey," she said as he threw back a palmful of the orange mints.

A sour look crossed his face, but it could've been from the overload of Tic Tacs. "Hey." He turned back to his friends, but he was clearly a fifth wheel with the family in front of him, and Renee seized onto that fact.

"What's your favorite ice cream?" she asked as she picked up a second bowl.

"I'm a purist," he said. "Vanilla bean." He bypassed the bananas too.

Renee didn't understand him at all, despite the orange Tic Tac connection. "No toppings?"

"I like caramel, chocolate, and pecans."

"Oh, pecans. Fancy." She trilled out a giggle, hoping to draw him into a real conversation once they made it through the line.

He stared at her for a moment past comfortable and inched down the line—toward the pastor.

Renee's heart seized, then started beating at triple-time. Her first impulse was to duck out of line, and fast. Only sheer desire for the money kept her in place at Justin's side. And the vanilla tub sat way down on the end of the ice cream bar.

"They've set tables up out on the lawn," she said. "Were you going to go out there?"

"I hadn't really thought about it." Justin looked at her and flashed her a smile. "Is there shade?"

She grinned full-force at him. "I saw some umbrellas on the way in."

He glanced over his shoulder to his friends, but they'd already gotten their ice cream and were sprinkling nuts and candies on them. They didn't seem to notice that he'd fallen behind. He turned back to her and scanned her from her wedge-sandaled feet to the top of her head. His features softened as he drank in her kinky-curled hair.

"Probably better than hanging out with my boss."

"Hello, Justin," Pastor Peters said. "Good to see you down here this evening."

"First day of good weather," Justin said. "My boss insisted we get off the ranch."

"How are things with the horses?"

"Good." Justin exhaled and a strange look passed through his eyes. "Good."

Pastor Peters focused on hers, his eyes pleasant if not a bit surprised. "Renee. Coming back for seconds?"

All her muscles seized. She couldn't seem to look away from Justin, who settled all his weight on his left foot, away from her, and waited for her explanation.

She couldn't say that she hadn't eaten her original bowl. Or that she'd come over here on a bet, simply because Justin was at the end of the line.

"I only had one bite," she finally managed to say. "My cousin—" Justin visibly flinched, but Renee plowed on. "I gave her my bowl for a friend."

Pastor Palmer didn't seem to have a problem with her rather lame explanation. He nodded and asked, "Mint chocolate chip again?"

"Yes, please." Relief tumbled through her when Justin's lip curled upward and he moved on to the hot fudge. Renee pressed her eyes closed and wondered how long it would take before she blurted out that she'd split the money with him if he'd just say he asked her out.

———

Can Justin take a chance with his heart when the woman of his dreams doesn't know what to do with it? Find out in **THE COWBOY'S CHALLENGE - available now in ebook, paperback, and audiobook!**

Brush Creek Cowboy (Book 1): Former rodeo champion and cowboy Walker Thompson trains horses at Brush Creek Horse Ranch, where he lives a simple life in his cabin with his ten-year-old son. A widower of six years, he's worked with Tess Wagner, a widow who came to Brush Creek to escape the turmoil of her life to give her seven-year-old son a slower pace of life. But Tess's breast cancer is back...

Walker will have to decide if he'd rather spend even a short time with Tess than not have her in his life at all. Tess wants to feel God's love and power, but can she discover and accept God's will in order to find her happy ending?

The Cowboy's Challenge (Book 2): Cowboy and professional roper Justin Jackman has found solitude at Brush Creek Horse Ranch, preferring his time with the animals he trains over dating. With two failed engagements in his past, he's not really interested in getting his heart stomped on again. But when flirty and fun Renee Martin picks him up at a church ice cream bar--on a bet, no less--he finds himself more than just a little interested. His Gen-X attitudes are attractive to her; her Millennial behaviors drive him nuts. Can Justin look past their differences and take a chance on another engagement?

A Cowboy Proposal (Book 3): Ted Caldwell has been a retired bronc rider for years, and he thought he was perfectly happy training horses to buck at Brush Creek Ranch. He was wrong. When he meets April Nox, who comes to the ranch to hide her pregnancy from all her friends back in Jackson Hole, Ted realizes he has a huge family-shaped hole in his life. April is embarrassed, heartbroken, and trying to find her extinguished faith. She's never ridden a horse and wants nothing to do with a cowboy ever again. Can Ted and April create a family of happiness and love from a tragedy?

A New Family for the Cowboy (Book 4): Blake Gibbons oversees all the agriculture at Brush Creek Horse Ranch, sometimes moonlighting as a general contractor. When he meets Erin Shields, new in town, at her aunt's bakery, he's instantly smitten. Erin moved to Brush Creek after a divorce that left her

penniless, homeless, and a single mother of three children under age eight. She's nowhere near ready to start dating again, but the longer Blake hangs around the bakery, the more she starts to like him. Can Blake and Erin find a way to blend their lifestyles and become a family?

The Cowboy and the Champion (Book 5): Emmett Graves has always had a positive outlook on life. He adores training horses to become barrel racing champions during the day and cuddling with his cat at night. Fresh off her professional rodeo retirement, Molly Brady comes to Brush Creek Horse Ranch as Emmett's protege. He's not thrilled, and she's allergic to cats. Oh, and she'd like to stay cowboy-free, thank you very much. But Emmett's about as cowboy as they come.... Can Emmett and Molly work together without falling in love?

Schooled by the Cowboy (Book 6): Grant Ford spends his days training cattle—when he's not camped out at the elementary school hoping to catch a glimpse of his ex-girlfriend. When principal Shannon Sharpe confronts him and asks him to stay away from the school, the spark between them is instant and hot. Shan-non's expecting a transfer very soon, but she also needs a summer outdoor coordinator—and Grant fits the bill. Just because he's handsome and everything Shannon's ever wanted in a cowboy husband means nothing. Will Grant and Shannon be able to survive the summer or will the Utah heat be too much for them to handle?

The Marine's Marriage: A Fuller Family Novel - Brush Creek Cowboys Romance (Book 1): Tate Benson can't believe he's come to Nowhere, Utah, to fix up a house that hasn't been inhabited in years. But he has. Because he's retired from the Marines and looking to start a life as a police officer in small-town Brush Creek. Wren Fuller has her hands full most days running her family's company. When Tate calls and demands a maid for that morning, she decides to have the calls forwarded to her cell and go help him out. She didn't know he was moving in next door, and she's completely unprepared for his handsomeness, his kind heart, and his wounded soul. **Can Tate and Wren weather a relationship when they're also next-door neighbors?**

The Firefighter's Fiancé: A Fuller Family Novel - Brush Creek Cowboys Romance (Book 2): Cora Wesley comes to Brush Creek, hoping to get some in-the-wild firefighting training as she prepares to put in her application to be a hotshot. When she meets Brennan Fuller, the spark between them is hot and 

instant. As they get to know each other, her deadline is constantly looming over them, and Brennan starts to wonder if he can break ranks in the family business. He's okay mowing lawns and hanging out with his brothers, but he dreams of being able to go to college and become a landscape architect, but he's just not sure it can be done. **Will Cora and Brennan be able to endure their trials to find true love?**

The Trooper's Treasure: A Fuller Family Novel - Brush Creek Cowboys Romance (Book 3): Dawn Fuller has made some mistakes in her life, and she's not proud of the way McDermott Boyd found her off the road one day last year. She's spent a hard year wrestling with her choices and trying to fix them, glad for McDermott's acceptance and friendship. He lost his wife years ago, done his best with his daughter, and now he's ready to move on. **Can McDermott help Dawn find a way past her former mistakes and down a path that leads to love, family, and happiness?**

The Detective's Date: A Fuller Family Novel - Brush Creek Cowboys Romance (Book 4): Dahlia Reid is one of the best detectives Brush Creek and the surrounding towns has ever had. She's given up on the idea of marriage—and pleasing her mother—and has dedicated herself fully to her job. Which is great, since one of the most  perplexing cases of her career has come to town. Kyler Fuller thinks he's finally ready to move past the woman who ghosted him years ago. He's cut his hair, and he's ready to start dating. Too bad every woman he's been out with is about as interesting as a lamppost—until Dahlia. He finds her beautiful, her quick wit a breath of fresh air, and her intelligence sexy. **Can Kyler and Dahlia use their faith to find a way through the obstacles threatening to keep them apart?**

The Paramedic's Partner: A Fuller Family Novel - Brush Creek Cowboys Romance (Book 5): Jazzy Fuller has always been overshadowed by her prettier, more popular twin, Fabiana. Fabi meets paramedic Max Robinson at the park and sets a date with him only to come down with the flu. So she convinces Jazzy to cut her hair and take her place on the date. And the spark between Jazzy and Max is hot and instant...if only he knew she wasn't her sister, Fabi.

Max drives the ambulance for the town of Brush Creek with is partner Ed Moon, and neither of them have been all that lucky in love. Until Max suggests to who he thinks is Fabi that they should double with Ed and Jazzy. They do, and Fabi is smitten with the steady, strong Ed Moon. **As each twin falls further and further in love with their respective paramedic, it becomes obvious they'll need to come clean about the switcheroo sooner rather than later...or risk losing their hearts.**

The Chief's Catch: A Fuller Family Novel - Brush Creek Cowboys Romance (Book 6): Berlin Fuller has struck out with the dating scene in Brush Creek more times than she cares to admit. When she makes a deal with her friends that they can choose the next man she goes out with, she didn't dream they'd pick surly Cole Fairbanks, the new Chief of Police.

His friends call him the Beast and challenge him to complete ten dates that summer or give up his bonus check. When Berlin approaches him, stuttering about the deal with her friends and claiming they don't actually have to go out, he's intrigued. As the summer passes, Cole finds himself burning both ends of the candle to keep up with his job and his new relationship. **When he unleashes the Beast one time too many, Berlin will have to decide if she can tame him or if she should walk away.**

Graham (Book 1): Graham Whittaker returns to Coral Canyon a few days after Christmas—after the death of his father. He takes over the energy company his dad built from the ground up and buys a high-end lodge to live in—only a mile from the home of his once-best friend, Laney McAllister. They were best friends once, but Laney's always entertained feelings for him, and spending so much time with him while they make Christmas memories puts her heart in danger of getting broken again...

Eli (Book 2): Since the death of his wife a few years ago, Eli Whittaker has been running from one job to another, unable to find somewhere for him and his son to settle. Meg Palmer is Stockton's nanny, and she comes with her boss, Eli, to the lodge, her long-time crush on the man no different in Wyoming than it was on the beach. When she confesses her feelings for him and gets nothing in return, she's crushed, embarrassed, and unsure if she can stay in Coral Canyon for Christmas. Then Eli starts to show some feelings for her too...

Andrew (Book 3): Andrew Whittaker is the public face for the Whittaker Brothers' family energy company, and with his older brother's robot about to be announced, he needs a press secretary to help him get everything ready and tour the state to make the announcements. When he's hit by a protest sign being carried by the company's biggest opponent, Rebecca Collings, he learns with a few clicks that she has the background they need. He offers her the job of press secretary when she thought she was going to be arrested, and not only because the spark between them in so hot Andrew can't see straight.

Can Becca and Andrew work together and keep their relationship a secret? Or will hearts break in this classic romance retelling reminiscent of *Two Weeks Notice*?

Beau (Book 4): Beau Whittaker has watched his brothers find love one by one, but every attempt he's made has ended in disaster. Lily Everett has been in the spotlight since childhood and has half a dozen platinum records with her two sisters. She's taking a break from the brutal music industry and hiding out in Wyoming while her ex-husband continues to cause trouble for her. When she hears of Beau Whittaker and what he offers his clients, she wants to meet him. Beau is instantly attracted to Lily, but he tried a relationship with his last client that left a scar that still hasn't healed...

Can Lily use the spirit of Christmas to discover what matters most? Will Beau open his heart to the possibility of love with someone so different from him?

Todd (Book 5): Todd Christopherson has just retired from the professional rodeo circuit and returned to his hometown of Coral Canyon. Problem is, he's got no family there anymore, no land, and no job. Not that he needs a job--he's got plenty of money from his illustrious career riding bulls.

Then Todd gets thrown during a routine horseback ride up the canyon, and his only support as he recovers physically is the beautiful Violet Everett. She's no nurse, but she does the best she can for the handsome cowboy. **Will she lose her heart to the billionaire bull rider? Can Todd trust that God led him to Coral Canyon...and Vi?**

Liam (Book 6): Rose Everett isn't sure what to do with her life now that her country music career is on hold. After all, with both of her sisters in Coral Canyon, and one about to have a baby, they're not making albums anymore.

Liam Murphy has been working for Doctors Without Borders, but he's back in the US now, and looking to start a new clinic in Coral Canyon, where he spent his summers.

When Rose wins a date with Liam in a bachelor auction, their relationship blooms and grows quickly. **Can Liam and Rose find a solution to their problems that doesn't involve one of them leaving Coral Canyon with a broken heart?**

Finn (Book 7): Her sons want her to be happy, but she's too old to be set up on a blind date...isn't she?

Amanda Whittaker has been looking for a second chance at love since the death of her husband several years ago. Finley Barber is a cowboy in every sense of the word. Born and raised on a racehorse farm in Kentucky, he's since moved to Dog Valley and started his own breeding stable for champion horses. He hasn't dated in years, and everything about Amanda makes him nervous.

Will Amanda take the leap of faith required to be with Finn? Or will he become just another boyfriend who doesn't make the cut?

Zach (Book 8): When Celia Abbott-Armstrong runs into a gorgeous cowboy at her best friend's wedding, she decides she's ready to start dating again.

But the cowboy is Zach Zuckerman, and the Zuckermans and Abbotts have been at war for generations.

Can Zach and Celia find a way to reconcile their family's differences so they can have a future together?

Rhett (Book 1): To save her business, she'll have to risk her heart. She needs a husband to be credible as a matchmaker. He wants to help a neighbor. **Will their fake marriage take them out of the friend zone?**

Tripp (Book 2): She needs a husband to keep her son. He's wanted to take their relationship to the next level, but she's always pushing him away. Will their trivial tie take them all the way to happily-ever-after?

Liam (Book 3): She's desperate to save her ranch. He wants to help her any way he can. Will their invented I-Do open doors that have previously been closed and lead to a happily-ever-after for both of them?

Jeremiah (Book 4): He wants to prove to his brothers that he's not broken. She just wants him. Will a fake marriage heal him or push her further away?

Wyatt (Book 5): To get her inheritance, she needs a husband. He's wanted to fly with her for ages. Can their pretend pledge turn into something real?

Skyler (Book 6): She needs a new last name to stay in school. He's willing to help a fellow student. Can this wanna-be wife show the playboy that some things should be taken seriously?

Micah (Book 7): They were just actors auditioning for a play. The marriage was just for the audition – until a clerical error results in a legal marriage. Can these two ex-lovers negotiate this new ground between them and achieve new roles in each other's lives?

Gideon (Book 8): It's 1971, and Gideon Walker is on the cutting edge of all the technology coming out of Texas. He has big dreams and wants to make something of himself. Then he meets Penny Aarons, and everything changes. He only has eyes for her, but she's got plans and dreams of her own...

Read this origin romance for Momma and Daddy from the Seven Sons series today!

Second Chance Ranch: A Three Rivers Ranch Romance™ (Book 1): After his deployment, injured and discharged Major Squire Ackerman returns to Three Rivers Ranch, wanting to forgive Kelly for ignoring him a decade ago. He'd like to provide the stable life she needs, but with old wounds opening and a ranch on the brink of financial collapse, it will take patience and faith to make their second chance possible.

Third Time's the Charm: A Three Rivers Ranch Romance™ (Book 2): First Lieutenant Peter Marshall has a truckload of debt and no way to provide for a family, but Chelsea helps him see past all the obstacles, all the scars. With so many unknowns, can Pete and Chelsea develop the love, acceptance, and faith needed to find their happily ever after?

Fourth and Long: A Three Rivers Ranch Romance™ (Book 3): Commander Brett Murphy goes to Three Rivers Ranch to find some rest and relaxation with his Army buddies. Having his ex-wife show up with a seven-year-old she claims is his son is anything but the R&R he craves. Kate needs to make amends, and Brett needs to find forgiveness, but are they too late to find their happily ever after?

Fifth Generation Cowboy: A Three Rivers Ranch Romance™ (Book 4): Tom Lovell has watched his friends find their true happiness on Three Rivers Ranch, but everywhere he looks, he only sees friends. Rose Reyes has been bringing her daughter out to the ranch for equine therapy for months, but it doesn't seem to be working. Her challenges with Mari are just as frustrating as ever. Could Tom be exactly what Rose needs? Can he remove his friendship blinders and find love with someone who's been right in front of him all this time?

Sixth Street Love Affair: A Three Rivers Ranch Romance™ (Book 5): After losing his wife a few years back, Garth Ahlstrom thinks he's ready for a second chance at love. But Juliette Thompson has a secret that could destroy their budding relationship. Can they find the strength, patience, and faith to make things work?

The Seventh Sergeant: A Three Rivers Ranch Romance™ (Book 6): Life has finally started to settle down for Sergeant Reese Sanders after his devastating injury overseas. Discharged from the Army and now with a good job at Courage Reins, he's finally found happiness—until a horrific fall puts him right back where he was years ago: Injured and depressed. Carly Watters, Reese's new veteran care coordinator, dislikes small towns almost as much as she loathes cowboys. But she finds herself faced with both when she gets assigned to Reese's case. Do they have the humility and faith to make their relationship more than professional?

Eight Second Ride: A Three Rivers Ranch Romance™ (Book 7): Ethan Greene loves his work at Three Rivers Ranch, but he can't seem to find the right woman to settle down with. When sassy yet vulnerable Brynn Bowman shows up at the ranch to recruit him back to the rodeo circuit, he takes a different approach with the barrel racing champion. His patience and newfound faith pay off when a friendship--and more--starts with Brynn. But she wants out of the rodeo circuit right when Ethan wants to rejoin. Can they find the path God wants them to take and still stay together?

The Ninth Inning: A Three Rivers Ranch Romance™ (Book 8): The Christmas season has never felt like such a burden to boutique owner Andrea Larsen. But with Mama gone and the holidays upon her, Andy finds herself wishing she hadn't been so quick to judge her former boyfriend, cowboy Lawrence Collins. Well, Lawrence hasn't forgotten about Andy either, and he devises a plan to get her out to the ranch so they can reconnect. Do they have the faith and humility to patch things up and start a new relationship?

Ten Days in Town: A Three Rivers Ranch Romance™ (Book 9): Sandy Keller is tired of the dating scene in Three Rivers. Though she owns the pancake house, she's looking for a fresh start, which means an escape from the town where she grew up. When her older brother's best friend, Tad Jorgensen, comes to town for the holidays, it is a balm to his weary soul. A helicopter tour guide who experienced a near-death experience, he's looking to start over too--but in Three Rivers. Can Sandy and Tad navigate their troubles to find the path God wants them to take--and discover true love--in only ten days?

Eleven Year Reunion: A Three Rivers Ranch Romance™ (Book 10): Pastry chef extraordinaire, Grace Lewis has moved to Three Rivers to help Heidi Ackerman open a bakery in Three Rivers. Grace relishes the idea of starting over in a town where no one knows about her failed cupcakery. She doesn't expect to run into her old high school boyfriend, Jonathan Carver. A carpenter working at Three Rivers Ranch, Jon's in town against his will. But with Grace now on the scene, Jon's thinking life in Three Rivers is suddenly looking up. But with her focus on baking and his disdain for small towns, can they make their eleven year reunion stick?

The Twelfth Town: A Three Rivers Ranch Romance™ (Book 11): Newscaster Taryn Tucker has had enough of life on-screen. She's bounced from town to town before arriving in Three Rivers, completely alone and completely anonymous-- just the way she now likes it. She takes a job cleaning at Three Rivers Ranch, hoping for a chance to figure out who she is and where God wants her. When she meets happy-go-lucky cowhand Kenny Stockton, she doesn't expect sparks to fly. Kenny's always been "the best friend" for his female friends, but the pull between him and Taryn can't be denied. Will they have the courage and faith necessary to make their opposite worlds mesh?

Lucky Number Thirteen: A Three Rivers Ranch Romance™ (Book 12): Tanner Wolf, a rodeo champion ten times over, is excited to be riding in Three Rivers for the first time since he left his philandering ways and found religion. Seeing his old friends Ethan and Brynn is therapuetic--until a terrible accident lands him in the hospital. With his rodeo career over, Tanner thinks maybe he'll stay in town--and it's not just because his nurse, Summer Hamblin, is the prettiest woman he's ever met. But Summer's the queen of first dates, and as she looks for a way to make a relationship with the transient rodeo star work Summer's not sure she has the fortitude to go on a second date. Can they find love among the tragedy?

The Curse of February Fourteenth: A Three Rivers Ranch Romance™ (Book 13): Cal Hodgkins, cowboy veterinarian at Bowman's Breeds, isn't planning to meet anyone at the masked dance in small-town Three Rivers. He just wants to get his bachelor friends off his back and sit on the sidelines to drink his punch. But when he sees a woman dressed in gorgeous butterfly wings and cowgirl boots with blue stitching, he's smitten. Too bad she runs away from the dance before he can get her name, leaving only her boot behind...

Fifteen Minutes of Fame: A Three Rivers Ranch Romance™ (Book 14): Navy Richards is thirty-five years of tired—tired of dating the same men, working a demanding job, and getting her heart broken over and over again. Her aunt has always spoken highly of the matchmaker in Three Rivers, Texas, so she takes a six-month sabbatical from her high-stress job as a pediatric nurse, hops on a bus, and meets with the matchmaker. Then she meets Gavin Redd. He's handsome, he's hardworking, and he's a cowboy. But is he an Aquarius too? Navy's not making a move until she knows for sure...

Sixteen Steps to Fall in Love: A Three Rivers Ranch Romance™ (Book 15): A chance encounter at a dog park sheds new light on the tall, talented Boone that Nicole can't ignore. As they get to know each other better and start to dig into each other's past, Nicole is the one who wants to run. This time from her growing admiration and attachment to Boone. From her aging parents. From herself.

But Boone feels the attraction between them too, and he decides he's tired of running and ready to make Three Rivers his permanent home. **Can Boone and Nicole use their faith to overcome their differences and find a happily-ever-after together?**

The Sleigh on Seventeenth Street: A Three Rivers Ranch Romance™ (Book 16): A cowboy with skills as an electrician tries a relationship with a down-on-her luck plumber. Can Dylan and Camila make water and electricity play nicely together this Christmas season? Or will they get shocked as they try to make their relationship work?

The First Lady of Three Rivers Ranch: A Three Rivers Ranch Romance™ (Book 17): Heidi Duffin has been dreaming about opening her own bakery since she was thirteen years old. She scrimped and saved for years to afford baking and pastry school in San Francisco. And now she only has one year left before she's a certified pastry chef. Frank Ackerman's father has recently retired, and he's taken over the largest cattle ranch in the Texas Panhandle. A horseman through and through, he's also nearing thirty-one and looking for someone to bring love and joy to a homestead that's been dominated by men for a decade. But when he convinces Heidi to come clean the cowboy cabins, she changes all that. But the siren's call of a bakery is still loud in Heidi's ears, even if she's also seeing a future with Frank. Can she rely on her faith in ways she's never had to before or will their relationship end when summer does?

Eighteen Bowties and Counting: A Three Rivers Ranch Romance™ (Book 18): He's her older brother's best friend and completely off-limits. She's got a way with horses...and a heart condition. Can Beau and Charlotte navigate close quarters to find their happily-ever-after?

Last Chance Ranch (Book 1): A cowgirl down on her luck hires a man who's good with horses and under the hood of a car. Can Hudson fine tune Scarlett's heart as they work together? Or will things backfire and make everything worse at Last Chance Ranch?

Last Chance Cowboy (Book 2): A billionaire cowboy without a home meets a woman who secretly makes food videos to pay her debts...Can Carson and Adele do more than fight in the kitchens at Last Chance Ranch?

Last Chance Wedding (Book 3): A female carpenter needs a husband just for a few days... Can Jeri and Sawyer navigate the minefield of a pretend marriage before their feelings become real?

Last Chance Reunion (Book 4): An Army cowboy, the woman he dated years ago, and their last chance at Last Chance Ranch... Can Dave and Sissy put aside hurt feelings and make their second chance romance work?

Last Chance Lake (Book 5): A former dairy farmer and the marketing director on the ranch have to work together to make the cow cuddling program a success. But can Karla let Cache into her life? Or will she keep all her secrets from him - and keep *him* a secret too?

Last Chance Christmas (Book 6): She's tired of having her heart broken by cowboys. He waited too long to ask her out. Can Lance fix things quickly, or will Amber leave Last Chance Ranch before he can tell her how he feels?

Craving the Cowboy (Book 1): Dwayne Carver is set to inherit his family's ranch in the heart of Texas Hill Country, and in order to keep up with his ranch duties and fulfill his dreams of owning a horse farm, he hires top trainer Felicity Lightburne. They get along great, and she can envision herself on this new farm—at least until her mother falls ill and she has to return to help her. Can Dwayne and Felicity work through their differences to find their happily-ever-after?

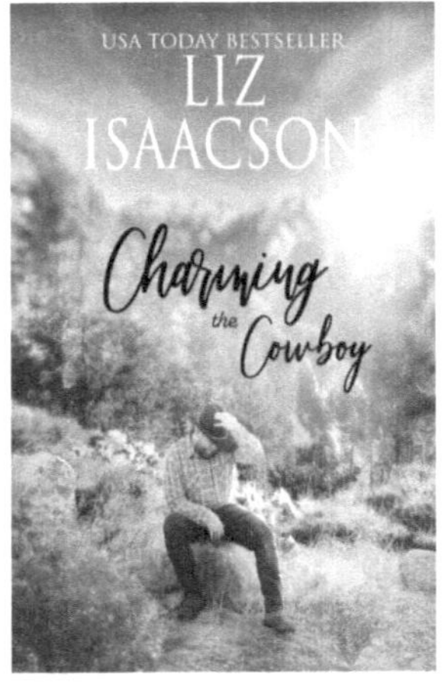

Charming the Cowboy (Book 2): Third grade teacher Heather Carver has had her eye on Levi Rhodes for a couple of years now, but he seems to be blind to her attempts to charm him. When she breaks her arm while on his horse ranch, Heather infiltrates Levi's life in ways he's never thought of, and his strict anti-female stance slips. Will Heather heal his emotional scars and he care for her physical ones so they can have a real relationship?

Courting the Cowboy (Book 3): Frustrated with the cowboy-only dating scene in Grape Seed Falls, May Sotheby joins Texas-Faithful.com, hoping to find her soul mate without having to relocate--or deal with cowboy hats and boots. She has no idea that Kurt Pemberton, foreman at Grape Seed Ranch, is the man she starts communicating with... Will May be able to follow her heart and get Kurt to forgive her so they can be together?

Claiming the Cowboy, Royal Brothers Book 1 (Grape Seed Falls Romance Book 4): Unwilling to be tied down, farrier Robin Cook has managed to pack her entire life into a two-hundred-and-eighty square-foot house, and that includes her Yorkie. Cowboy and co-foreman, Shane Royal has had his heart set on Robin for three years, even though she flat-out turned him down the last time he asked her to dinner. But she's back at Grape Seed Ranch for five weeks as she works her horseshoeing magic, and he's still interested, despite a bitter life lesson that left a bad taste for marriage in his mouth.

Robin's interested in him too. But can she find room for Shane in her tiny house--and can he take a chance on her with his tired heart?

Catching the Cowboy, Royal Brothers Book 2 (Grape Seed Falls Romance Book 5): Dylan Royal is good at two things: whistling and caring for cattle. When his cows are being attacked by an unknown wild animal, he calls Texas Parks & Wildlife for help. He wasn't expecting a beautiful mammologist to show up, all flirty and fun and everything Dylan didn't know he wanted in his life.

Hazel Brewster has gone on more first dates than anyone in Grape Seed Falls, and she thinks maybe Dylan deserves a second... Can they find their way through wild animals, huge life changes, and their emotional pasts to find their forever future?

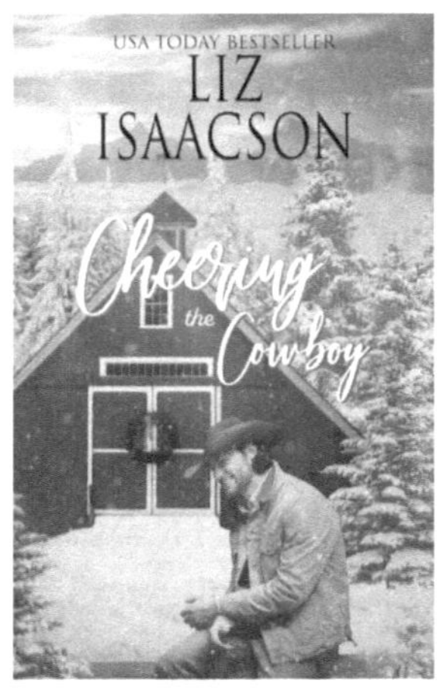

Cheering the Cowboy, Royal Brothers Book 3 (Grape Seed Falls Romance Book 6): Austin Royal loves his life on his new ranch with his brothers. But he doesn't love that Shayleigh Hatch came with the property, nor that he has to take the blame for the fact that he now owns her childhood ranch. They rarely have a conversation that doesn't leave him furious and frustrated--and yet he's still attracted to Shay in a strange, new way.

Shay inexplicably likes him too, which utterly confuses and angers her. As they work to make this Christmas the best the Triple Towers Ranch has ever seen, can they also navigate through their rocky relationship to smoother waters?

Choosing the Cowboy (Book 7): With financial trouble and personal issues around every corner, can Maggie Duffin and Chase Carver rely on their faith to find their happily-ever-after?

A spinoff from the #1 bestselling Three Rivers Ranch Romance novels, also by USA Today bestselling author Liz Isaacson.

Her Billionaire Cowboy (Book 1): Tucker Jenkins has had enough of tall buildings, traffic, and has traded in his technology firm in New York City for Steeple Ridge Horse Farm in rural Vermont. Missy Marino has worked at the farm since she was a teen, and she's always dreamed of owning it. But her ex-husband left her with a truckload of debt, making her fantasies of owning the farm unfulfilled. Tucker didn't come to the country to find a new wife, but he supposes a woman could help him start over in Steeple Ridge. Will Tucker and Missy be able to navigate the shaky ground between them to find a new beginning?

Her Restless Cowboy: A Butters Brothers Novel, Steeple Ridge Romance (Book 2): Ben Buttars is the youngest of the four Buttars brothers who come to Steeple Ridge Farm, and he finally feels like he's landed somewhere he can make a life for himself. Reagan Cantwell is a decade older than Ben and the recreational direction for the town of Island Park. Though Ben is young, he knows what he wants—and that's Rae. Can she figure out how to put what matters most in her life—family and faith—above her job before she loses Ben?

Her Faithful Cowboy: A Butters Brothers Novel, Steeple Ridge Romance (Book 3): Sam Buttars has spent the last decade making sure he and his brothers stay together. They've been at Steeple Ridge for a while now, but with the youngest married and happy, the siren's call to return to his parents' farm in Wyoming is loud in Sam's ears. He'd just go if it weren't for beautiful Bonnie Sherman, who roped his heart the first time he saw her. Do Sam and Bonnie have the faith to find comfort in each other instead of in the people who've already passed?

Her Mistletoe Cowboy: A Butters Brothers Novel, Steeple Ridge Romance (Book 4): Logan Buttars has always been good-natured and happy-go-lucky. After watching two of his brothers settle down, he recognizes a void in his life he didn't know about. Veterinarian Layla Guyman has appreciated Logan's friendship and easy way with animals when he comes into the clinic to get the service dogs. But with his future at Steeple Ridge in the balance, she's not sure a relationship with him is worth the risk. Can she rely on her faith and employ patience to tame Logan's wild heart?

Her Patient Cowboy: A Butters Brothers Novel, Steeple Ridge Romance (Book 5): Darren Buttars is cool, collected, and quiet—and utterly devastated when his girlfriend of nine months, Farrah Irvine, breaks up with him because he wanted her to ride her horse in a parade. But Farrah doesn't ride anymore, a fact she made very clear to Darren. She returned to her childhood home with so much baggage, she doesn't know where to start with the unpacking. Darren's the only Buttars brother who isn't married, and he wants to make Island Park his permanent home—with Farrah. Can they find their way through the heartache to achieve a happily-ever-after together?

The Redesigned Ranch (Book 1): Jace Lovell, still nursing a wounded heart after being jilted at the altar, has dedicated himself to becoming the best foreman at Horseshoe Home Ranch. When he decides to hire an interior designer to please the ranch owner's wife, he didn't expect to be faced with a familiar face from his past. **Can Belle's patience and faith help Jace find the path to forgiveness and lead them to discover their own slice of happily-ever-after?**

Snowed in with the Cowboy (Book 2): Sterling Maughan, once a renowned snowboarder, is in self-imposed exile at his family cabin after a tragic accident stole his career. Lost and without purpose, solitude is his only companion until an unexpected visitor disrupts his isolation. **Can Norah trust Sterling enough to let him into her life and give their unexpected and forbidden love a chance?**

The Preacher's Daughter (Book 3): Landon Edmunds, a cowboy born and bred, has had his rodeo dreams realized and then dashed by a career-ending injury. Back in his hometown working at Horseshoe Home Ranch, he yearns for a new beginning with a ranch of his own. His sights are set on buying a horse ranch to train rodeo horses, but his plans take a detour when his high school best friend, Megan Palmer, steps back into his life. **Will they choose to follow their hearts, or will they let true love slip through their fingers again?**

Be sure to check out the spinoff series, the Brush Creek Cowboys romances after you read THE PREACHER'S DAUGHTER. Start with BRUSH CREEK COWBOY.

The Cowboy and the Nanny(Book 4): Twelve years ago, Owen Carr traded his roots and his sweetheart in Gold Valley for the bright lights of Nashville, where he found fame as a country music star. But when a tragic accident leaves him single-handedly raising his eight-year-old niece, Marie, he's forced to return home. Overwhelmed and out of his depth, Owen finds a lifeline in a most unexpected place. **As they mend bridges and explore the sparks that still sizzle between them, will they open their hearts to a second chance at love?**

Right Cowboy, Right Time (Book 5): Caleb Chamberlain, a fun-loving cowboy at Horseshoe Home Ranch, has spent the last five years wrestling with the ghosts of his past—a devastating breakup, alcoholism, and a near-fatal accident. Now, he's finally found solace in laughter and the rhythmic simplicity of ranch life. But a chance encounter with a familiar face threatens to upheave his newfound peace. **Can they navigate the shadows of the past to find their happily-ever-after?**

Second Chance Family (Book 6): Ty Barker has been living a carefree existence for the last thirty years. As friends around him found love and started families, Ty filled his time by giving horseback riding lessons and serving on a community service committee. But beneath the jovial surface, he's starting to feel the sting of loneliness. **He knows he wants River Lee in his life—but the question is, can he navigate the delicate steps needed to make her stay with him?**

The Christmas Cowboy Competition (Book 7): Archer Bailey has already had to yield one job to Emersyn "Emery" Enders. So when the opportunity of a cowhand job at Horseshoe Home Ranch presents itself, he keeps it to himself. Emery, whose temporary job is ending but whose responsibilities towards her physically disabled sister aren't, is left in the dark.

As the festive season unfolds, **will Emery and Archer navigate the complexities of the ranch, their close living arrangements, and their personal challenges to discover the love building between them? Or will their rivalry rob them of the greatest Christmas gift of all—true love?**

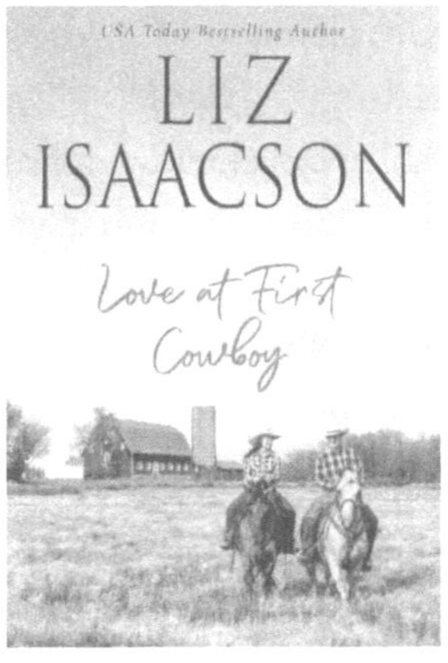

Love at First Cowboy (Book 8): Elliott Hawthorne, a career cowboy, has just witnessed his best friend and cabinmate forsake bachelorhood for matrimony. He'd be joyous if he weren't so green with envy. When a call about a family accident demands his presence, Elliott finds himself rushing from the ranch to his parents' house to see what's going on with his daddy, where he encounters the most stunning woman he's ever laid eyes on. **But as they encounter the complex dynamics of family responsibilities and personal desires, can their love-at-first-sight grow strong enough withstand the test of time?**

About Liz

Liz Isaacson writes inspirational romance, usually set in Texas, or Wyoming, or anywhere else horses and cowboys exist. She lives in Utah, where she writes full-time, takes her two dogs to the park everyday, and eats a lot of veggies while writing. Find her on her website at feelgoodfiction-books.com